Melusine

Love Potions

Written by: GILSON
Illustrated by: CLARKE
Colour work: Cerise

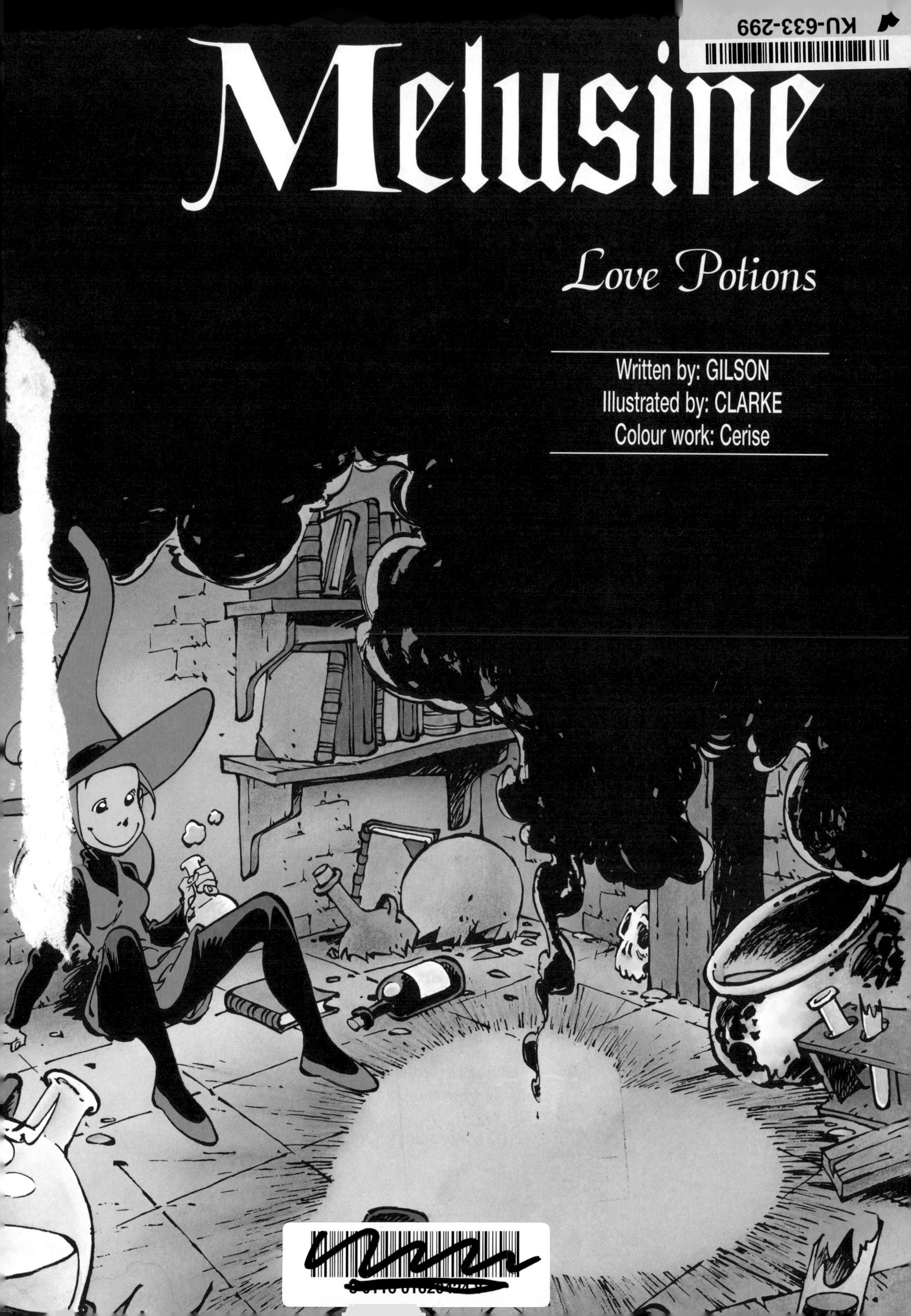

Original title: Mélusine 5 – Philtres d'amour

Original edition: © Dupuis, 1998
by Clarke & Gilson
www.dupuis.com
All rights reserved

English translation: © 2009 Cinebook Ltd

Translator: Jerome Saincantin
Lettering and text layout: Imadjinn
Printed in Spain by Just Colour Graphic

This edition first published in Great Britain in 2009 by
Cinebook Ltd
56 Beech Avenue
Canterbury, Kent
CT4 7TA
www.cinebook.com

A CIP catalogue record for this book
is available from the British Library

ISBN 978-1-84918-005-4

9th CINEBOOK
The 9th Art Publisher

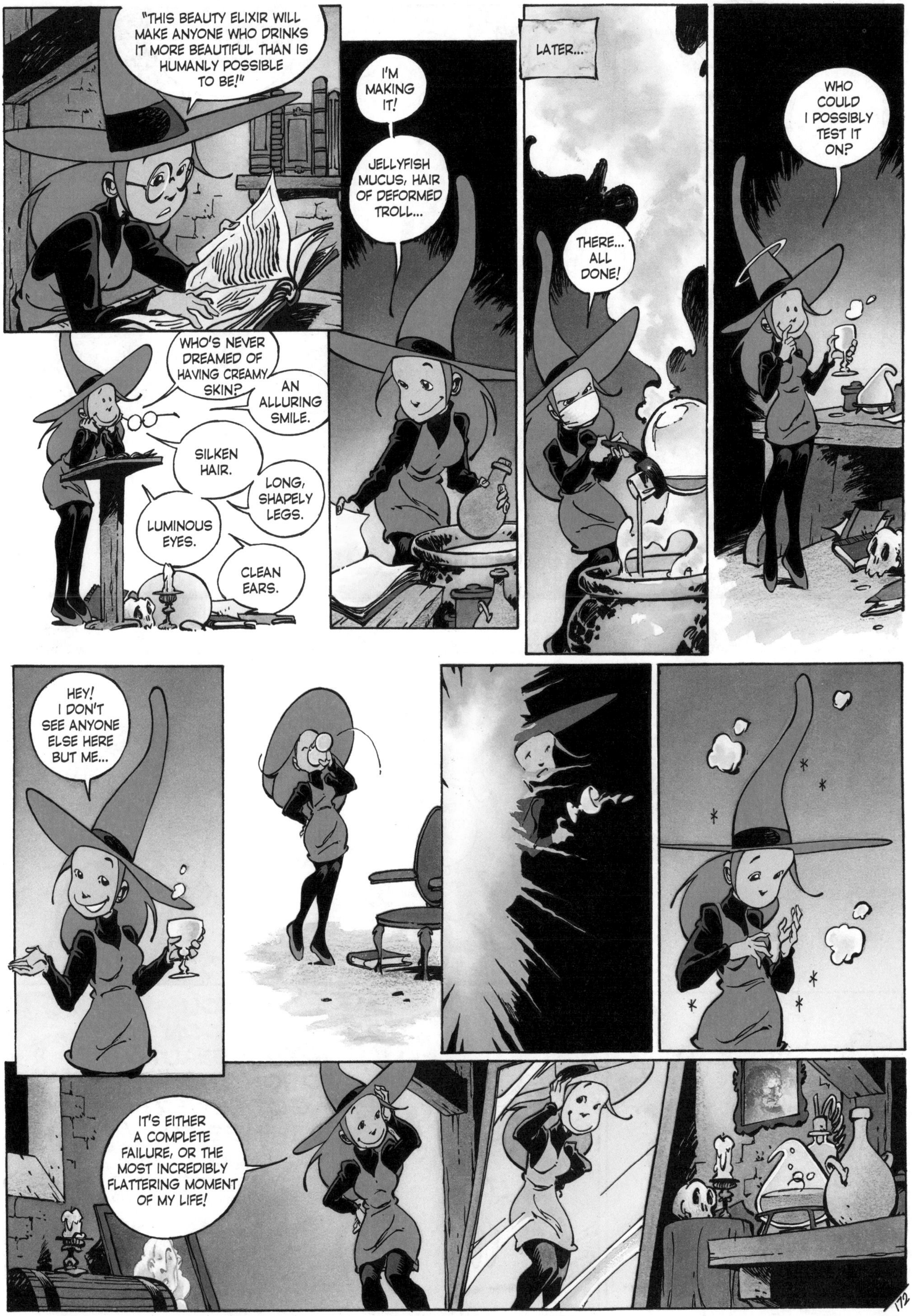
"THIS BEAUTY ELIXIR WILL MAKE ANYONE WHO DRINKS IT MORE BEAUTIFUL THAN IS HUMANLY POSSIBLE TO BE!"
WHO'S NEVER DREAMED OF HAVING CREAMY SKIN?
AN ALLURING SMILE.
SILKEN HAIR.
LONG, SHAPELY LEGS.
LUMINOUS EYES.
CLEAN EARS.
I'M MAKING IT!
JELLYFISH MUCUS, HAIR OF DEFORMED TROLL...
LATER...
THERE... ALL DONE!
WHO COULD I POSSIBLY TEST IT ON?
HEY! I DON'T SEE ANYONE ELSE HERE BUT ME...
IT'S EITHER A COMPLETE FAILURE, OR THE MOST INCREDIBLY FLATTERING MOMENT OF MY LIFE!

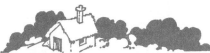

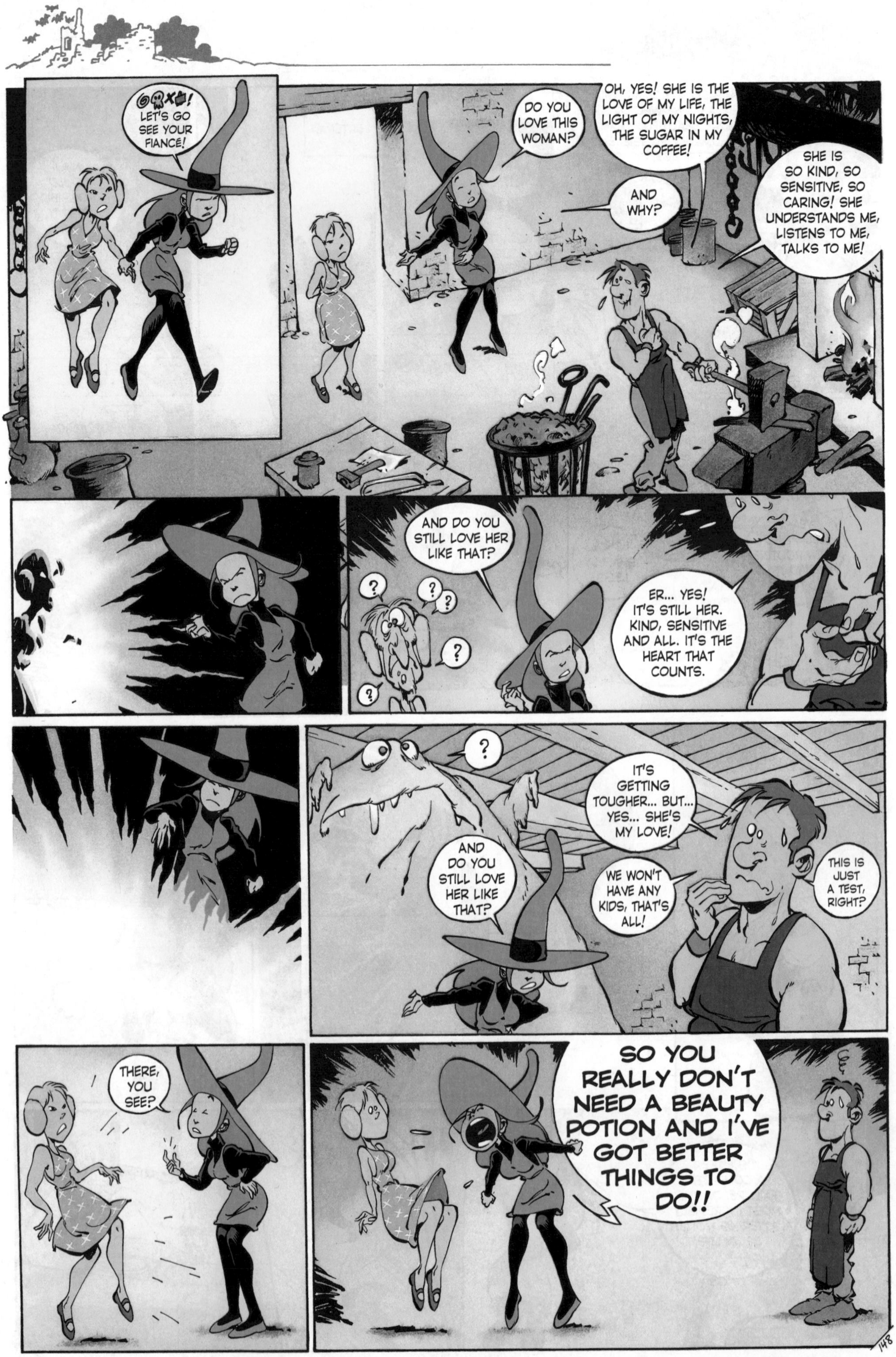

@§x$!
LET'S GO SEE YOUR FIANCÉ!
DO YOU LOVE THIS WOMAN?
OH, YES! SHE IS THE LOVE OF MY LIFE, THE LIGHT OF MY NIGHTS, THE SUGAR IN MY COFFEE!
AND WHY?
SHE IS SO KIND, SO SENSITIVE, SO CARING! SHE UNDERSTANDS ME, LISTENS TO ME, TALKS TO ME!
AND DO YOU STILL LOVE HER LIKE THAT?
?
?
?
?
?
ER... YES! IT'S STILL HER. KIND, SENSITIVE AND ALL. IT'S THE HEART THAT COUNTS.
?
IT'S GETTING TOUGHER... BUT... YES... SHE'S MY LOVE!
AND DO YOU STILL LOVE HER LIKE THAT?
WE WON'T HAVE ANY KIDS, THAT'S ALL!
THIS IS JUST A TEST, RIGHT?
THERE, YOU SEE?
SO YOU REALLY DON'T NEED A BEAUTY POTION AND I'VE GOT BETTER THINGS TO DO!!
148

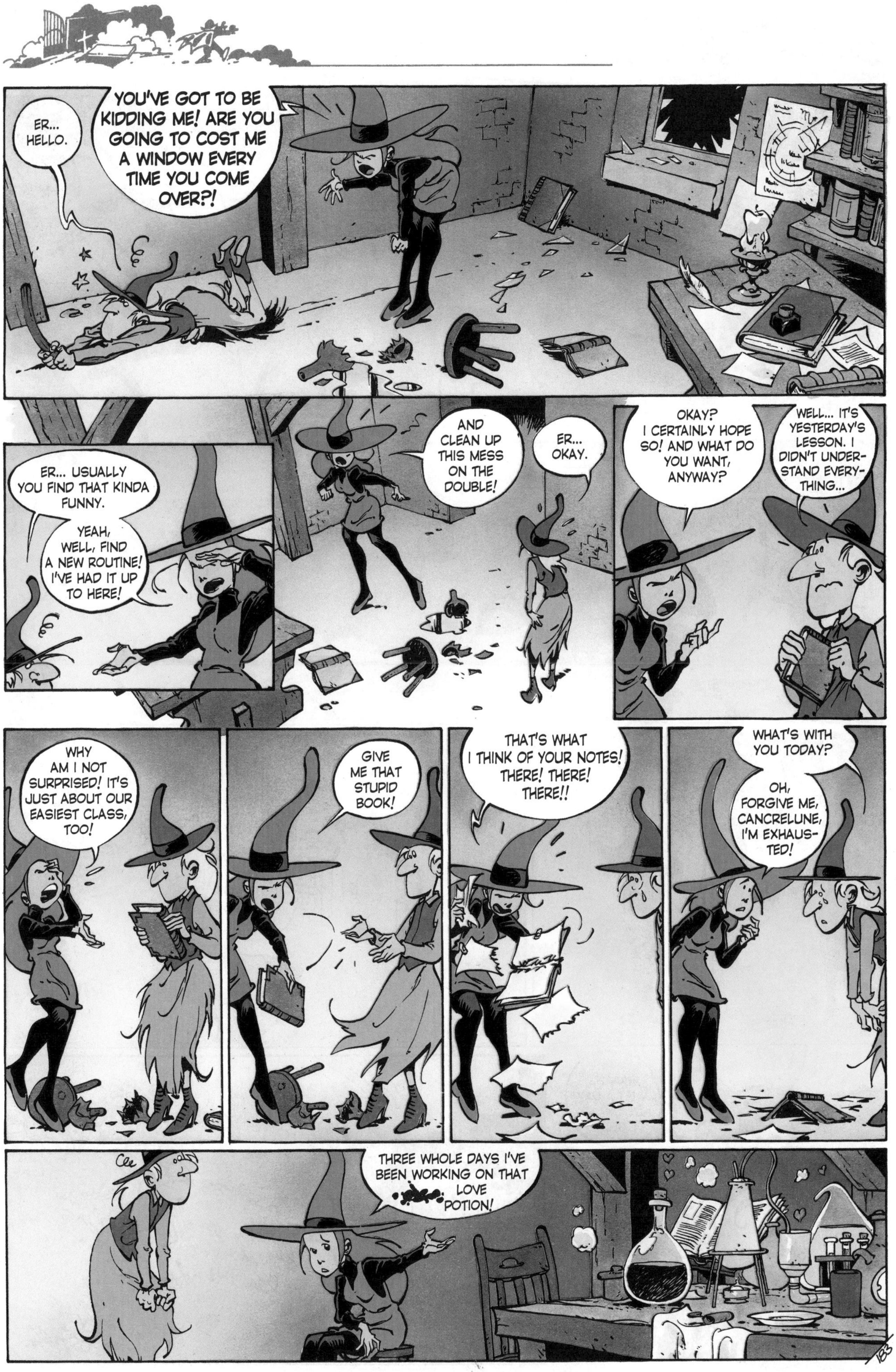
ER... HELLO.
YOU'VE GOT TO BE KIDDING ME! ARE YOU GOING TO COST ME A WINDOW EVERY TIME YOU COME OVER?!
ER... USUALLY YOU FIND THAT KINDA FUNNY.
YEAH, WELL, FIND A NEW ROUTINE! I'VE HAD IT UP TO HERE!
AND CLEAN UP THIS MESS ON THE DOUBLE!
ER... OKAY.
OKAY? I CERTAINLY HOPE SO! AND WHAT DO YOU WANT, ANYWAY?
WELL... IT'S YESTERDAY'S LESSON. I DIDN'T UNDER-STAND EVERY-THING...
WHY AM I NOT SURPRISED! IT'S JUST ABOUT OUR EASIEST CLASS, TOO!
GIVE ME THAT STUPID BOOK!
THAT'S WHAT I THINK OF YOUR NOTES! THERE! THERE! THERE!!
WHAT'S WITH YOU TODAY?
OH, FORGIVE ME, CANCRELUNE, I'M EXHAUS-TED!
THREE WHOLE DAYS I'VE BEEN WORKING ON THAT LOVE POTION!

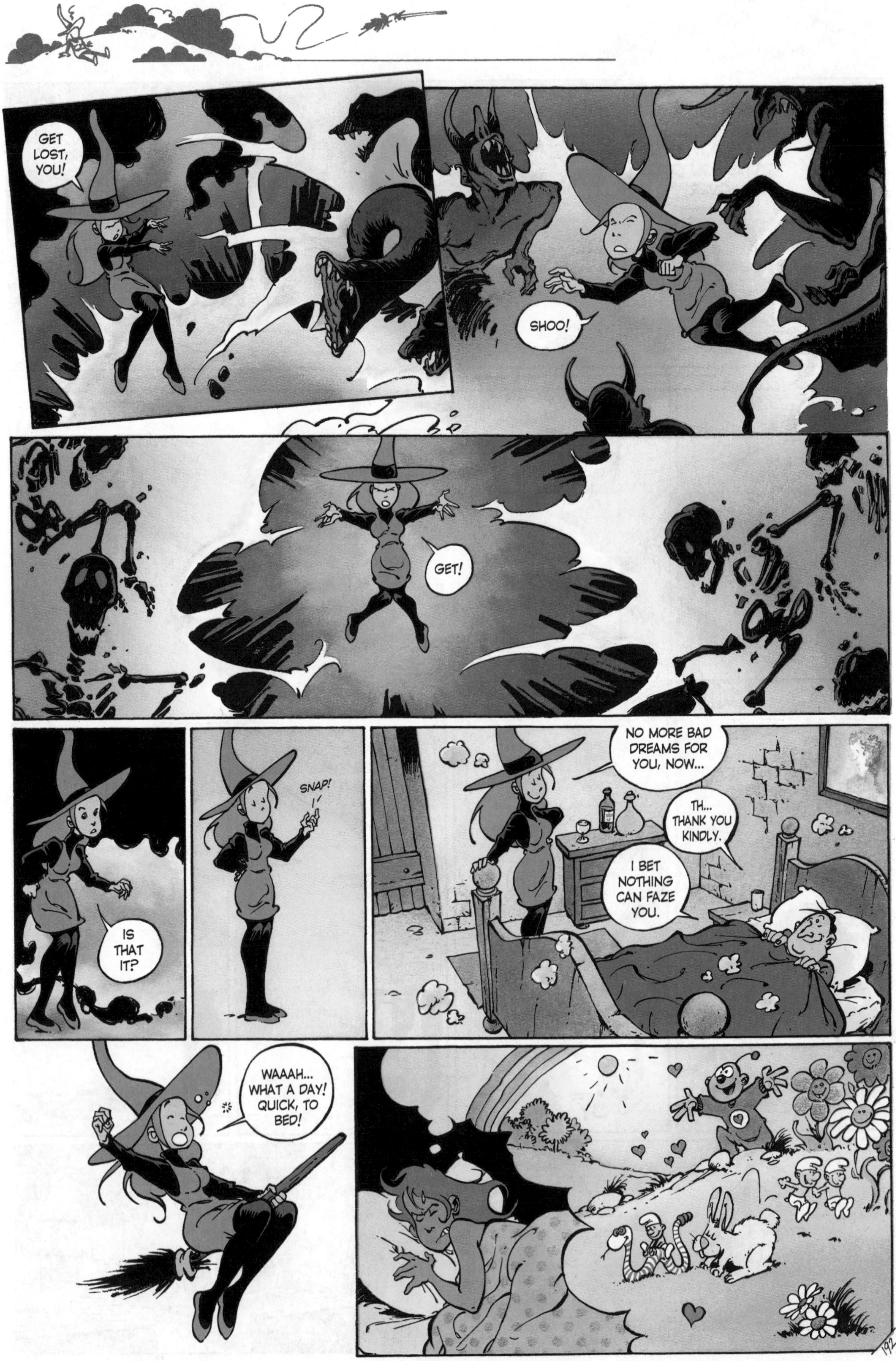
GET LOST, YOU!
SHOO!
GET!
IS THAT IT?
SNAP!
NO MORE BAD DREAMS FOR YOU, NOW...
TH... THANK YOU KINDLY.
I BET NOTHING CAN FAZE YOU.
WAAAH... WHAT A DAY! QUICK, TO BED!

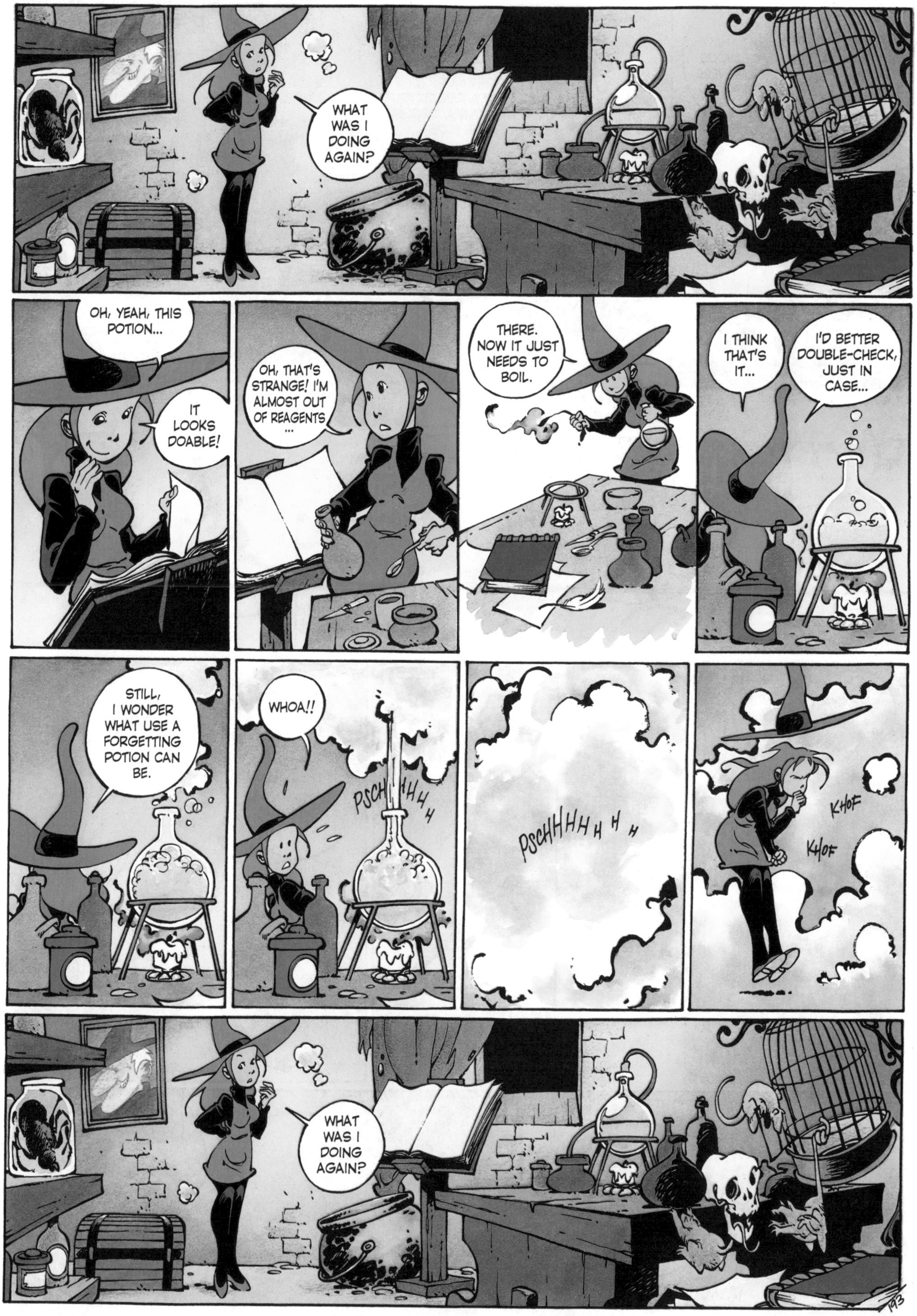
WHAT WAS I DOING AGAIN?
OH, YEAH, THIS POTION...
IT LOOKS DOABLE!
OH, THAT'S STRANGE! I'M ALMOST OUT OF REAGENTS ...
THERE. NOW IT JUST NEEDS TO BOIL.
I THINK THAT'S IT...
I'D BETTER DOUBLE-CHECK, JUST IN CASE...
STILL, I WONDER WHAT USE A FORGETTING POTION CAN BE.
WHOA!!
PSCHHHHH
PSCHHHHHHH
KHOF
KHOF
WHAT WAS I DOING AGAIN?

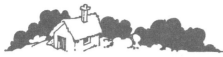

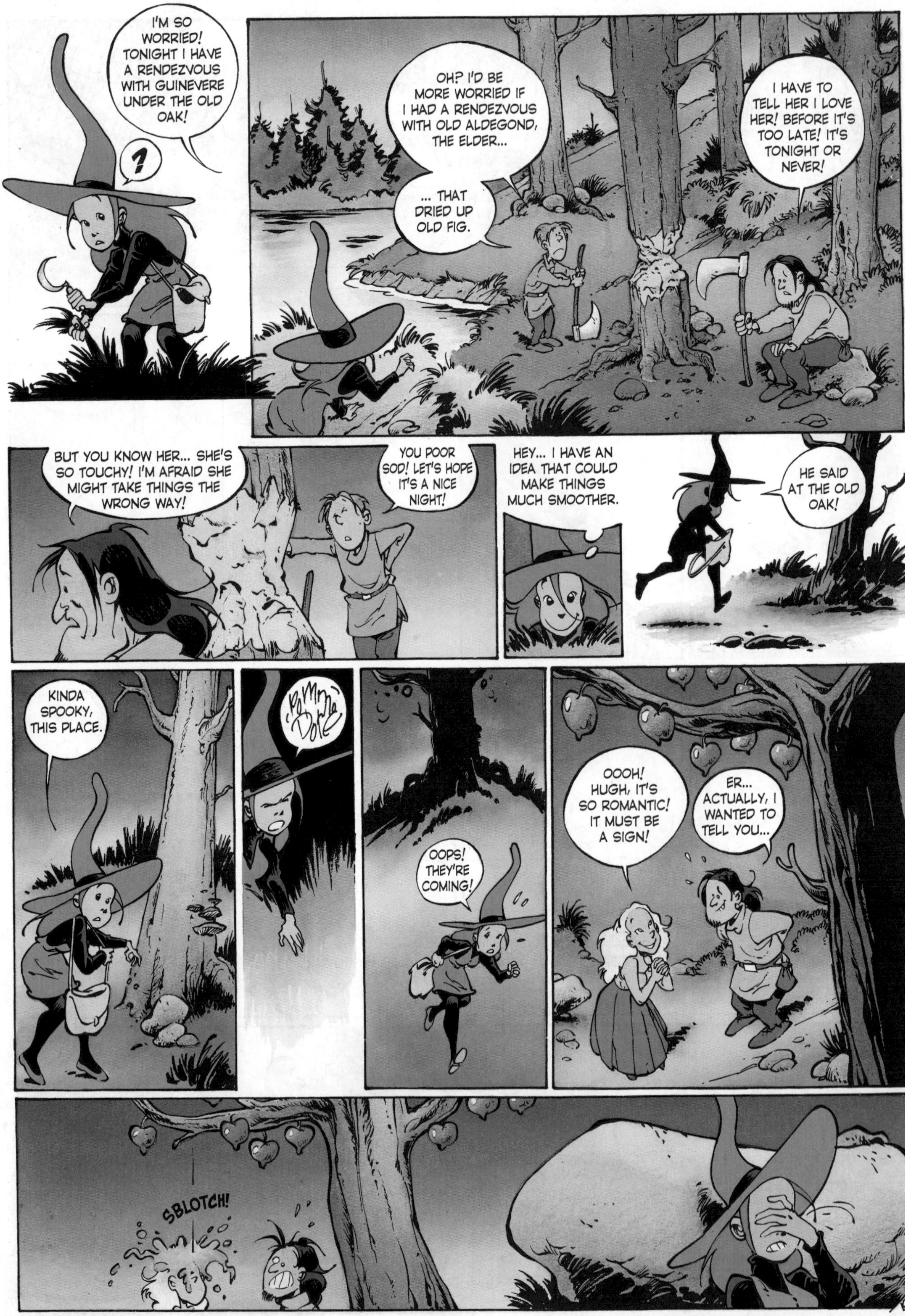
I'M SO WORRIED! TONIGHT I HAVE A RENDEZVOUS WITH GUINEVERE UNDER THE OLD OAK!
?
OH? I'D BE MORE WORRIED IF I HAD A RENDEZVOUS WITH OLD ALDEGOND, THE ELDER...
... THAT DRIED UP OLD FIG.
I HAVE TO TELL HER I LOVE HER! BEFORE IT'S TOO LATE! IT'S TONIGHT OR NEVER!
BUT YOU KNOW HER... SHE'S SO TOUCHY! I'M AFRAID SHE MIGHT TAKE THINGS THE WRONG WAY!
YOU POOR SOD! LET'S HOPE IT'S A NICE NIGHT!
HEY... I HAVE AN IDEA THAT COULD MAKE THINGS MUCH SMOOTHER.
HE SAID AT THE OLD OAK!
KINDA SPOOKY, THIS PLACE.
OOPS! THEY'RE COMING!
OOOH! HUGH, IT'S SO ROMANTIC! IT MUST BE A SIGN!
ER... ACTUALLY, I WANTED TO TELL YOU...
SBLOTCH!

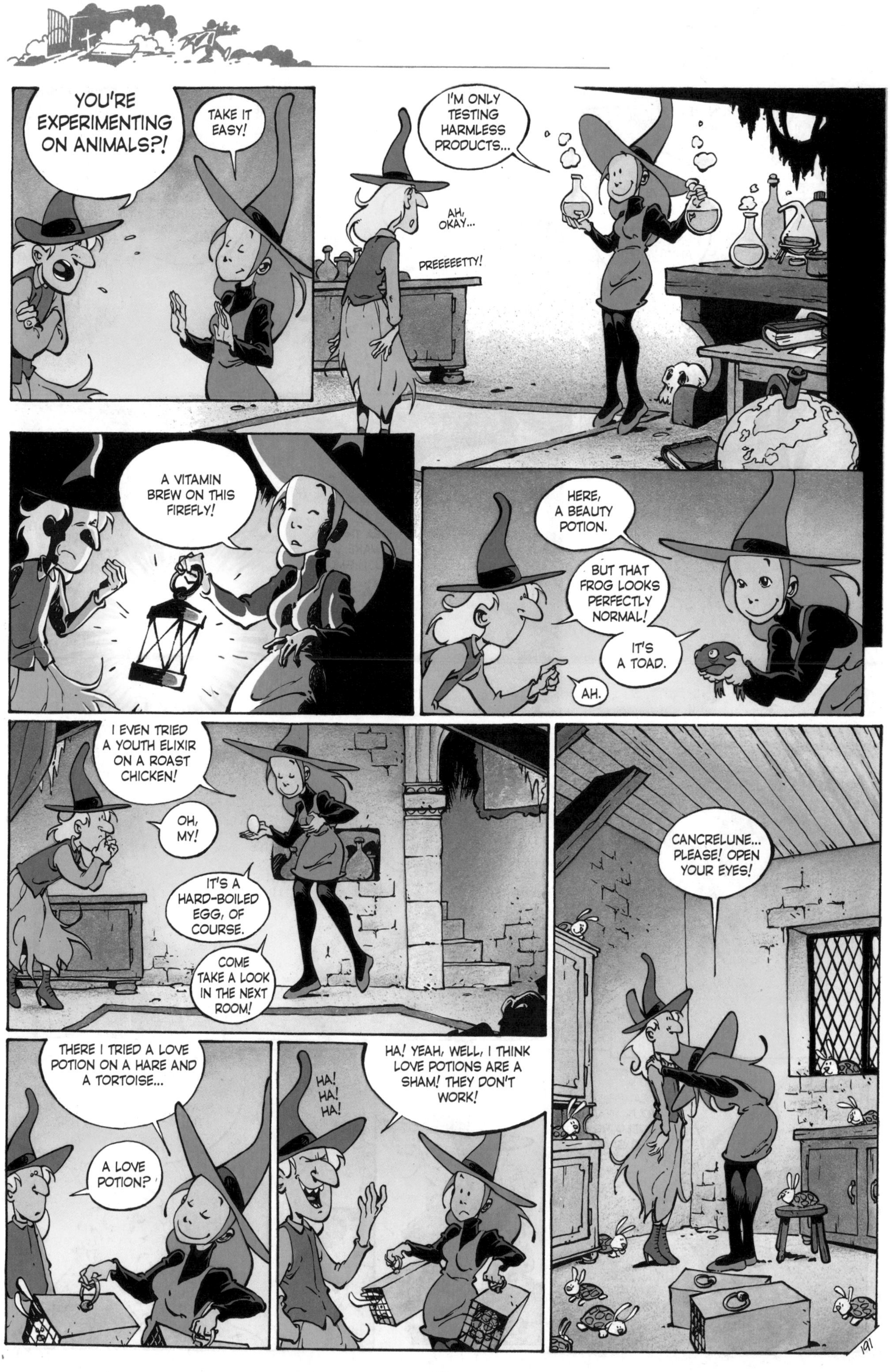

YOU'RE EXPERIMENTING ON ANIMALS?!
TAKE IT EASY!
I'M ONLY TESTING HARMLESS PRODUCTS...
AH, OKAY...
PREEEEETTY!
A VITAMIN BREW ON THIS FIREFLY!
HERE, A BEAUTY POTION.
BUT THAT FROG LOOKS PERFECTLY NORMAL!
IT'S A TOAD.
AH.
I EVEN TRIED A YOUTH ELIXIR ON A ROAST CHICKEN!
OH, MY!
IT'S A HARD-BOILED EGG, OF COURSE.
COME TAKE A LOOK IN THE NEXT ROOM!
CANCRELUNE... PLEASE! OPEN YOUR EYES!
THERE I TRIED A LOVE POTION ON A HARE AND A TORTOISE...
A LOVE POTION?
HA! HA! HA!
HA! YEAH, WELL, I THINK LOVE POTIONS ARE A SHAM! THEY DON'T WORK!

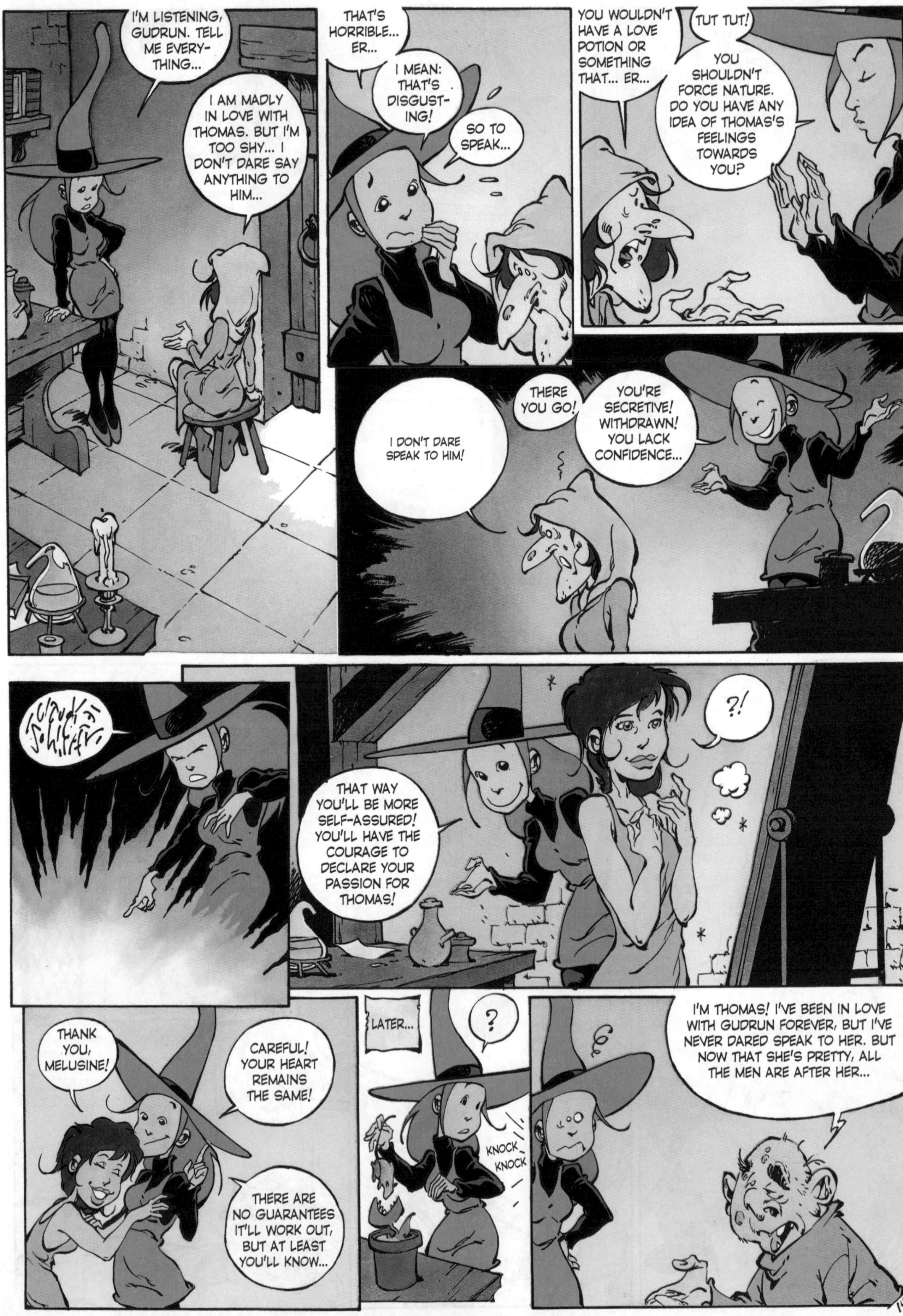

I'M LISTENING, GUDRUN. TELL ME EVERY-THING...
I AM MADLY IN LOVE WITH THOMAS. BUT I'M TOO SHY... I DON'T DARE SAY ANYTHING TO HIM...
THAT'S HORRIBLE... ER...
I MEAN: THAT'S DISGUST-ING!
SO TO SPEAK...
YOU WOULDN'T HAVE A LOVE POTION OR SOMETHING THAT... ER...
TUT TUT!
YOU SHOULDN'T FORCE NATURE. DO YOU HAVE ANY IDEA OF THOMAS'S FEELINGS TOWARDS YOU?
I DON'T DARE SPEAK TO HIM!
THERE YOU GO!
YOU'RE SECRETIVE! WITHDRAWN! YOU LACK CONFIDENCE...
?!
THAT WAY YOU'LL BE MORE SELF-ASSURED! YOU'LL HAVE THE COURAGE TO DECLARE YOUR PASSION FOR THOMAS!
THANK YOU, MELUSINE!
CAREFUL! YOUR HEART REMAINS THE SAME!
THERE ARE NO GUARANTEES IT'LL WORK OUT, BUT AT LEAST YOU'LL KNOW...
LATER...
?
KNOCK KNOCK
I'M THOMAS! I'VE BEEN IN LOVE WITH GUDRUN FOREVER, BUT I'VE NEVER DARED SPEAK TO HER. BUT NOW THAT SHE'S PRETTY, ALL THE MEN ARE AFTER HER...

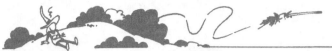

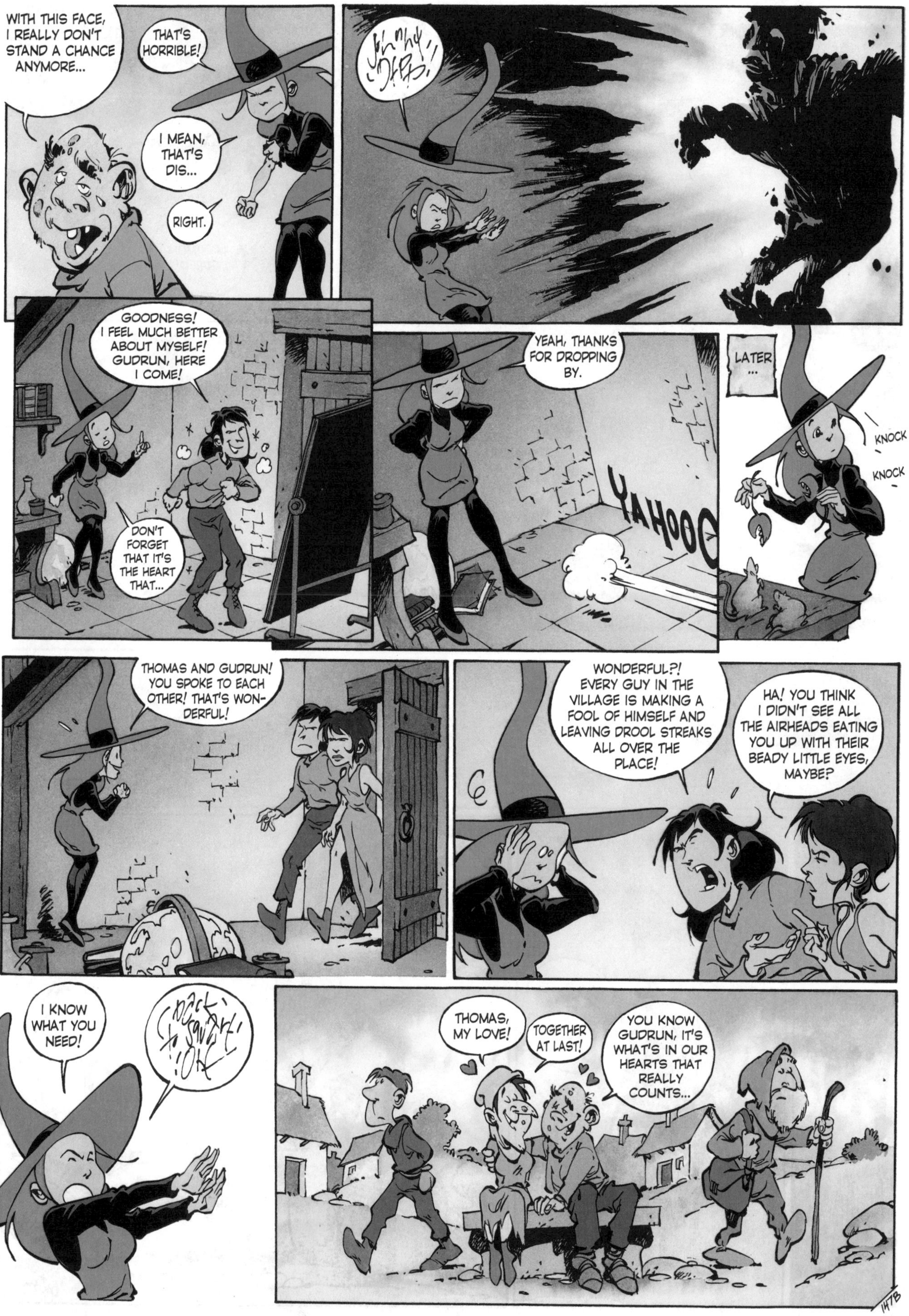

WITH THIS FACE, I REALLY DON'T STAND A CHANCE ANYMORE...
THAT'S HORRIBLE!
I MEAN, THAT'S DIS...
RIGHT.
GOODNESS! I FEEL MUCH BETTER ABOUT MYSELF! GUDRUN, HERE I COME!
DON'T FORGET THAT IT'S THE HEART THAT...
YEAH, THANKS FOR DROPPING BY.
YAHOOO
LATER...
KNOCK
KNOCK
THOMAS AND GUDRUN! YOU SPOKE TO EACH OTHER! THAT'S WONDERFUL!
WONDERFUL?! EVERY GUY IN THE VILLAGE IS MAKING A FOOL OF HIMSELF AND LEAVING DROOL STREAKS ALL OVER THE PLACE!
HA! YOU THINK I DIDN'T SEE ALL THE AIRHEADS EATING YOU UP WITH THEIR BEADY LITTLE EYES, MAYBE?
I KNOW WHAT YOU NEED!
THOMAS, MY LOVE!
TOGETHER AT LAST!
YOU KNOW GUDRUN, IT'S WHAT'S IN OUR HEARTS THAT REALLY COUNTS...

HEY? THAT'S MY NIECE OVER THERE!

WHOA! SHE DROPPED SOMETHING!

MAXIMUM SPEED!

GOT IT! HA! HA! HA! THIS OLD TIMER'S STILL GOT IT!

HEY-HO, MELUSINE! YOU DROPPED A VIAL WITH A FUSE!

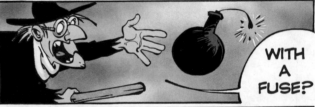

WITH A FUSE?

BM!

A MIXTURE OF COAL, SULPHUR AND SALTPETRE...

... A LITTLE TREAT FOR BUTANE, THE DRAGON I'M TRYING TO TAME!

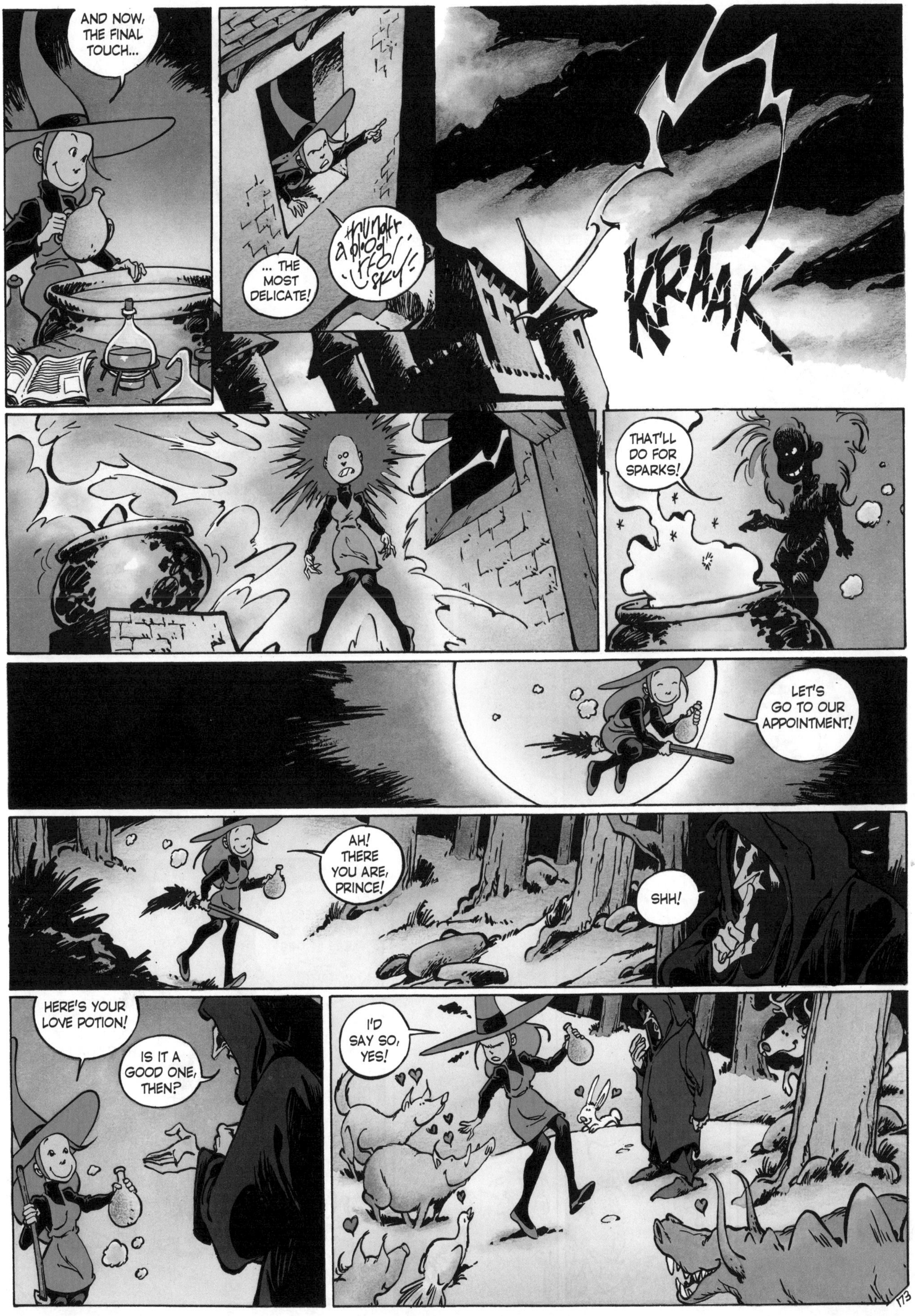
AND NOW, THE FINAL TOUCH...
... THE MOST DELICATE!
KRAAK
THAT'LL DO FOR SPARKS!
LET'S GO TO OUR APPOINTMENT!
AH! THERE YOU ARE, PRINCE!
SHH!
HERE'S YOUR LOVE POTION!
IS IT A GOOD ONE, THEN?
I'D SAY SO, YES!

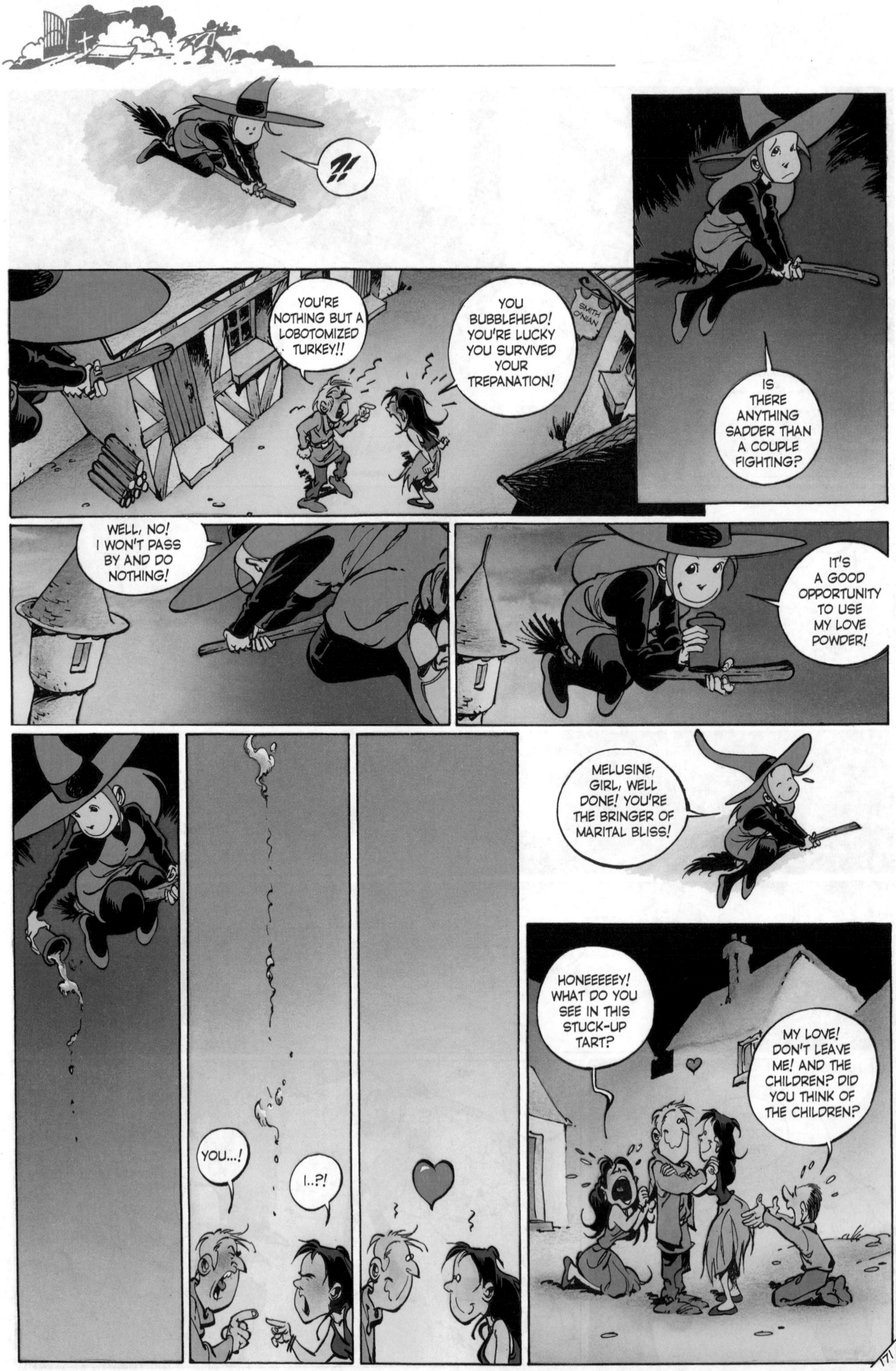
?!
YOU'RE NOTHING BUT A LOBOTOMIZED TURKEY!!
YOU BUBBLEHEAD! YOU'RE LUCKY YOU SURVIVED YOUR TREPANATION!
SMITH O'NIAN
IS THERE ANYTHING SADDER THAN A COUPLE FIGHTING?
WELL, NO! I WON'T PASS BY AND DO NOTHING!
IT'S A GOOD OPPORTUNITY TO USE MY LOVE POWDER!
YOU...!
I..?!
MELUSINE, GIRL, WELL DONE! YOU'RE THE BRINGER OF MARITAL BLISS!
HONEEEEEY! WHAT DO YOU SEE IN THIS STUCK-UP TART?
MY LOVE! DON'T LEAVE ME! AND THE CHILDREN? DID YOU THINK OF THE CHILDREN?

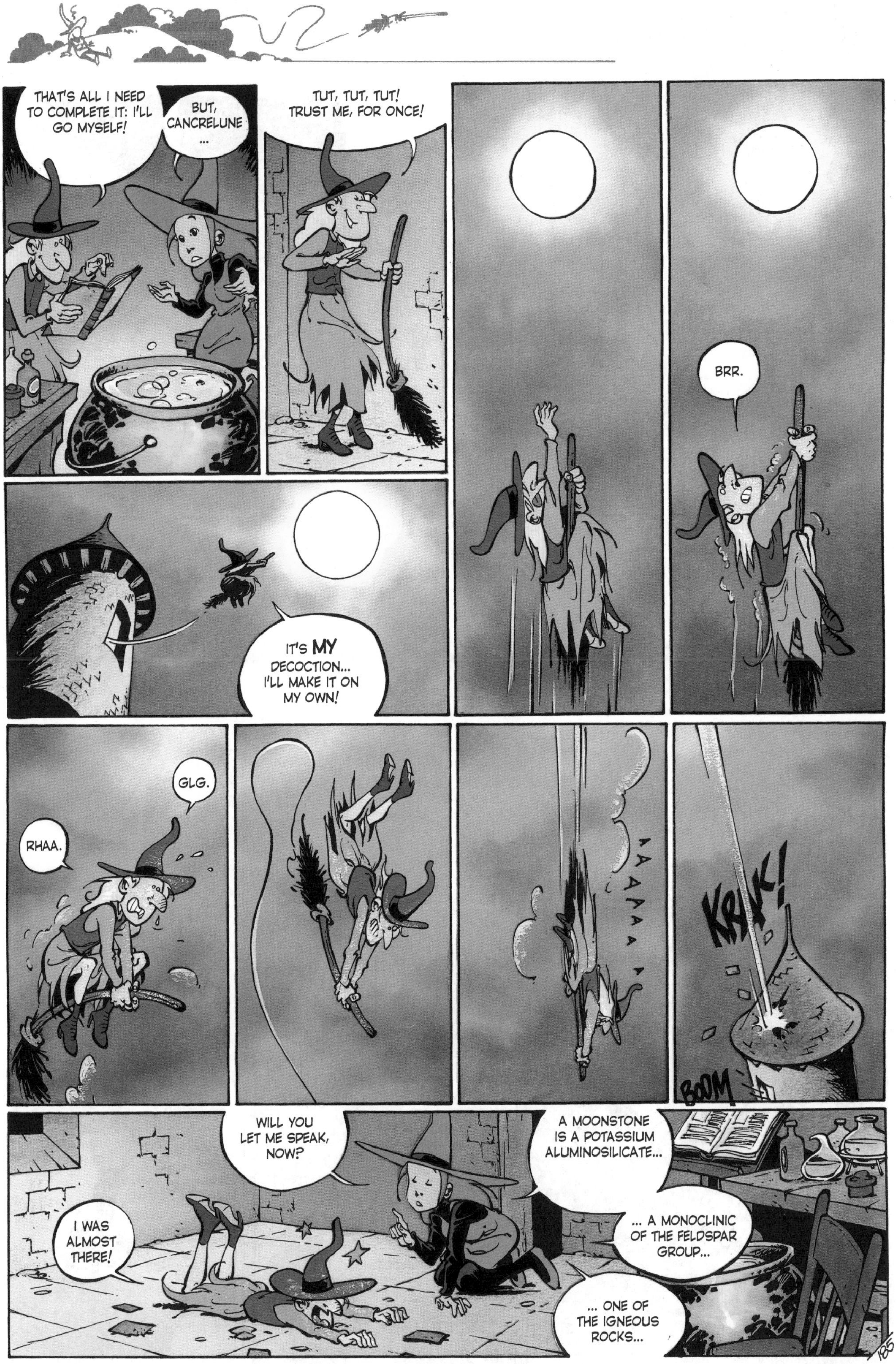
THAT'S ALL I NEED TO COMPLETE IT: I'LL GO MYSELF!
BUT, CANCRELUNE ...
TUT, TUT, TUT! TRUST ME, FOR ONCE!
BRR.
IT'S MY DECOCTION... I'LL MAKE IT ON MY OWN!
GLG.
RHAA.
AAAAAAAA
KRAK!
BOOM
WILL YOU LET ME SPEAK, NOW?
I WAS ALMOST THERE!
A MOONSTONE IS A POTASSIUM ALUMINOSILICATE...
... A MONOCLINIC OF THE FELDSPAR GROUP...
... ONE OF THE IGNEOUS ROCKS...

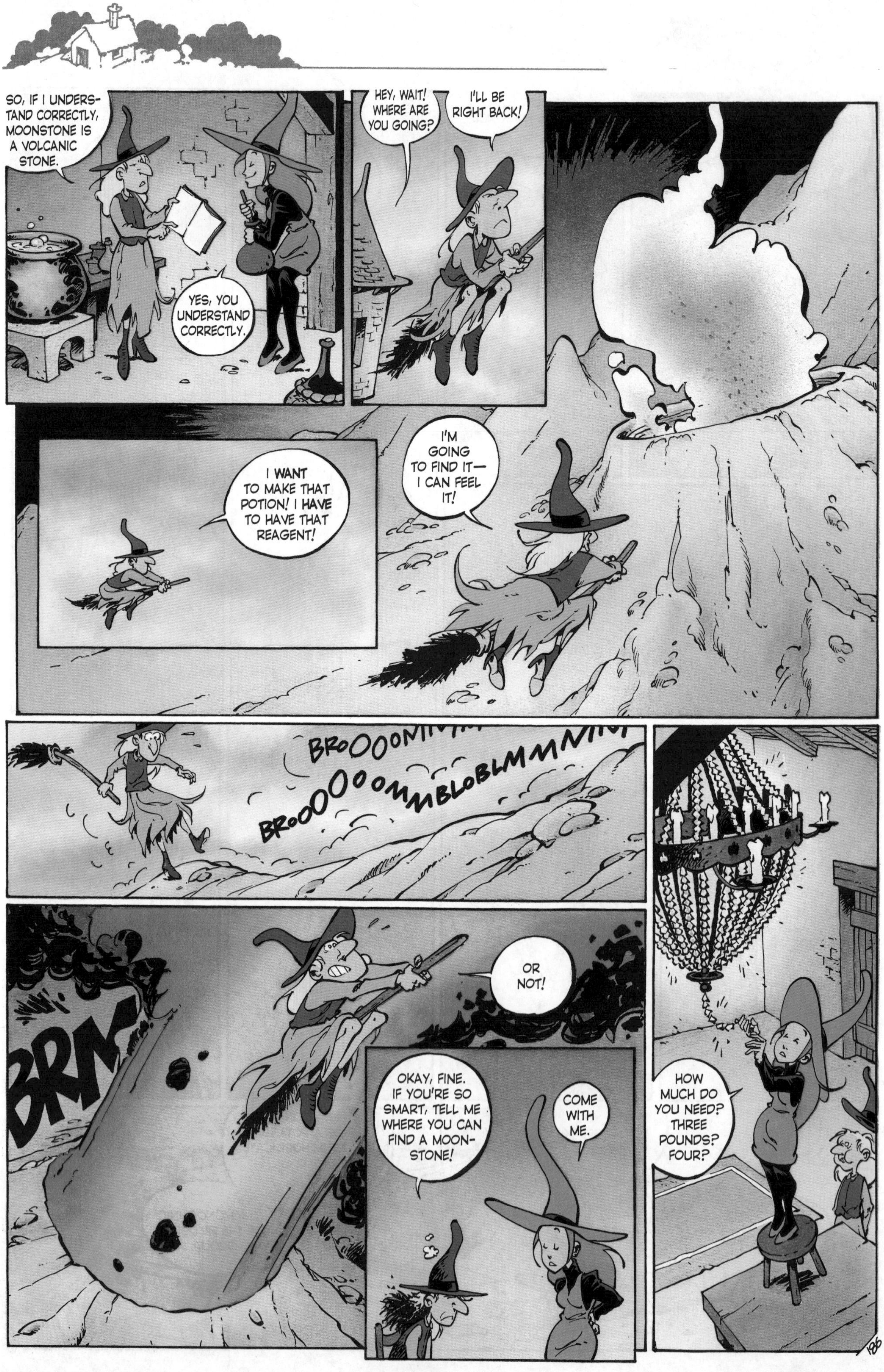
SO, IF I UNDERSTAND CORRECTLY, MOONSTONE IS A VOLCANIC STONE.
YES, YOU UNDERSTAND CORRECTLY.
HEY, WAIT! WHERE ARE YOU GOING?
I'LL BE RIGHT BACK!
I WANT TO MAKE THAT POTION! I HAVE TO HAVE THAT REAGENT!
I'M GOING TO FIND IT— I CAN FEEL IT!
BROOOOMMMM
BROOOOOMMBLOBLMMMM
BRM
OR NOT!
OKAY, FINE. IF YOU'RE SO SMART, TELL ME WHERE YOU CAN FIND A MOONSTONE!
COME WITH ME.
HOW MUCH DO YOU NEED? THREE POUNDS? FOUR?

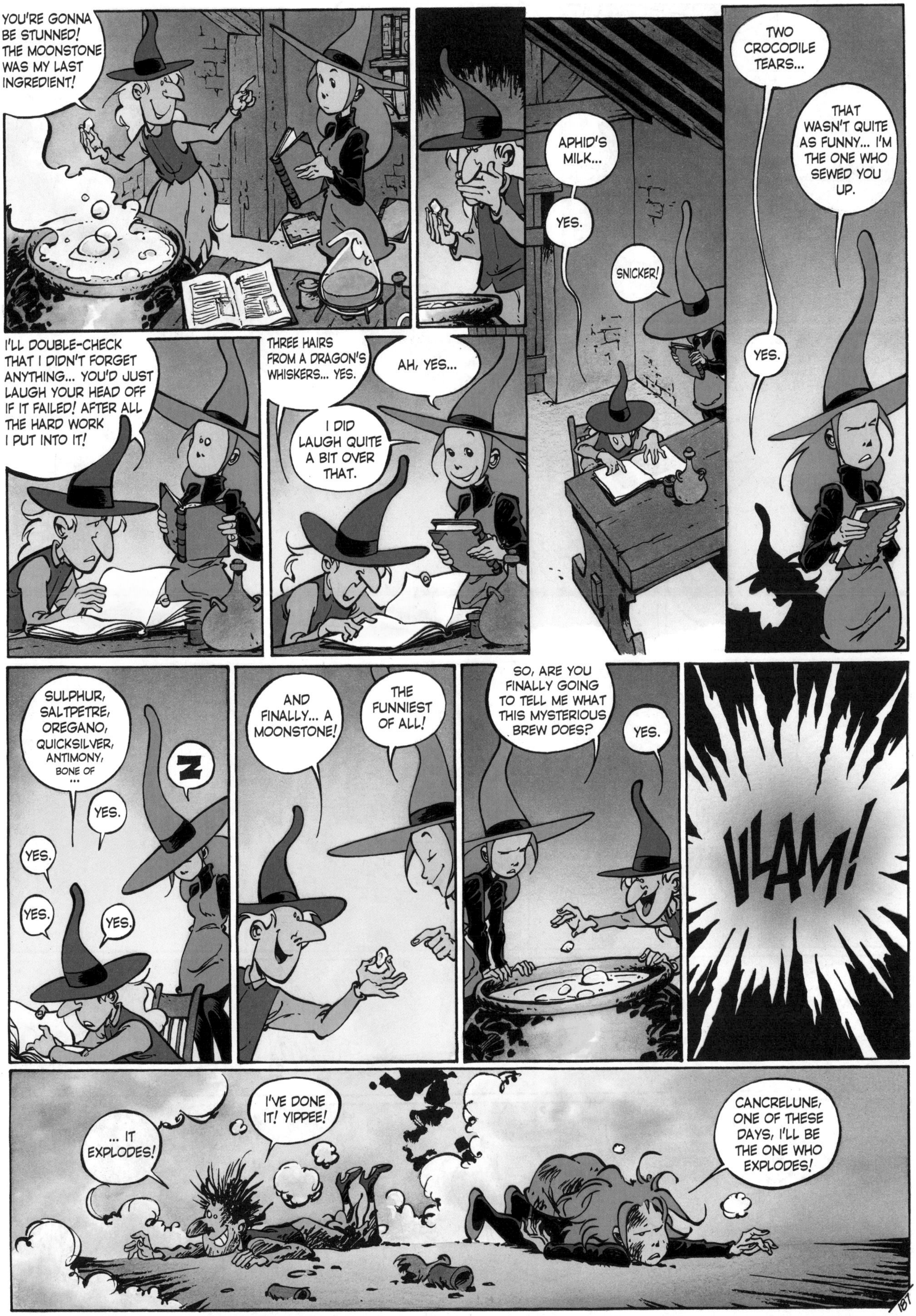
YOU'RE GONNA BE STUNNED! THE MOONSTONE WAS MY LAST INGREDIENT!
APHID'S MILK...
YES.
SNICKER!
TWO CROCODILE TEARS...
THAT WASN'T QUITE AS FUNNY... I'M THE ONE WHO SEWED YOU UP.
YES.
I'LL DOUBLE-CHECK THAT I DIDN'T FORGET ANYTHING... YOU'D JUST LAUGH YOUR HEAD OFF IF IT FAILED! AFTER ALL THE HARD WORK I PUT INTO IT!
THREE HAIRS FROM A DRAGON'S WHISKERS... YES.
AH, YES...
I DID LAUGH QUITE A BIT OVER THAT.
SULPHUR, SALTPETRE, OREGANO, QUICKSILVER, ANTIMONY, BONE OF ...
Z
YES.
YES.
YES.
YES.
AND FINALLY... A MOONSTONE!
THE FUNNIEST OF ALL!
SO, ARE YOU FINALLY GOING TO TELL ME WHAT THIS MYSTERIOUS BREW DOES?
YES.
VLAM!
... IT EXPLODES!
I'VE DONE IT! YIPPEE!
CANCRELUNE, ONE OF THESE DAYS, I'LL BE THE ONE WHO EXPLODES!

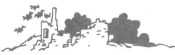

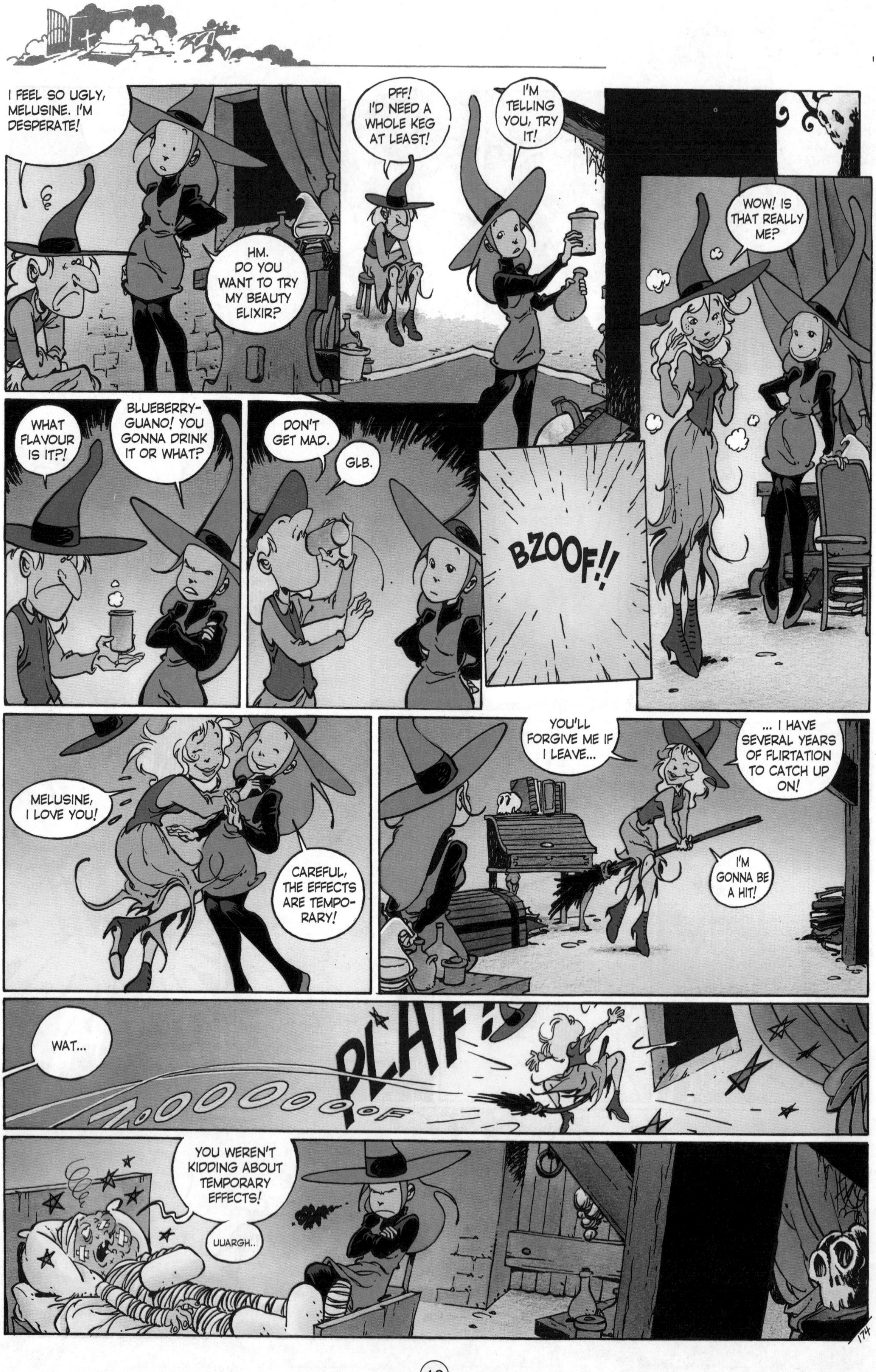
I FEEL SO UGLY, MELUSINE. I'M DESPERATE!
HM. DO YOU WANT TO TRY MY BEAUTY ELIXIR?
PFF! I'D NEED A WHOLE KEG AT LEAST!
I'M TELLING YOU, TRY IT!
WOW! IS THAT REALLY ME?
WHAT FLAVOUR IS IT?!
BLUEBERRY-GUANO! YOU GONNA DRINK IT OR WHAT?
DON'T GET MAD.
GLB.
BZOOF!!
MELUSINE, I LOVE YOU!
CAREFUL, THE EFFECTS ARE TEMPO-RARY!
YOU'LL FORGIVE ME IF I LEAVE...
... I HAVE SEVERAL YEARS OF FLIRTATION TO CATCH UP ON!
I'M GONNA BE A HIT!
WAT...
ZOOOOOOOOOF
PLAF!
YOU WEREN'T KIDDING ABOUT TEMPORARY EFFECTS!
UUARGH..
174

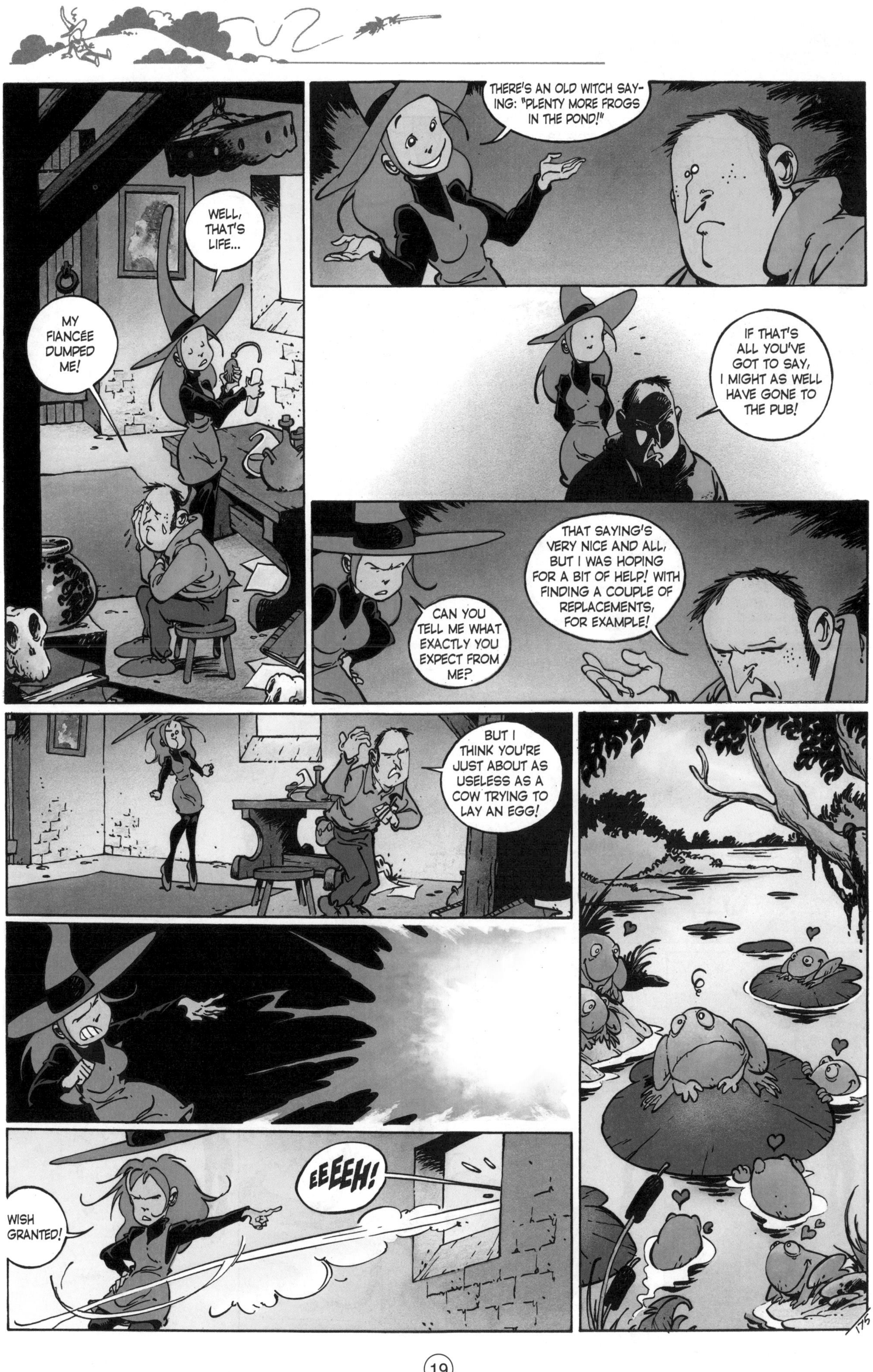
MY FIANCÉE DUMPED ME!
WELL, THAT'S LIFE...
THERE'S AN OLD WITCH SAYING: "PLENTY MORE FROGS IN THE POND!"
IF THAT'S ALL YOU'VE GOT TO SAY, I MIGHT AS WELL HAVE GONE TO THE PUB!
THAT SAYING'S VERY NICE AND ALL, BUT I WAS HOPING FOR A BIT OF HELP! WITH FINDING A COUPLE OF REPLACEMENTS, FOR EXAMPLE!
CAN YOU TELL ME WHAT EXACTLY YOU EXPECT FROM ME?
BUT I THINK YOU'RE JUST ABOUT AS USELESS AS A COW TRYING TO LAY AN EGG!
EEEEH!
WISH GRANTED!

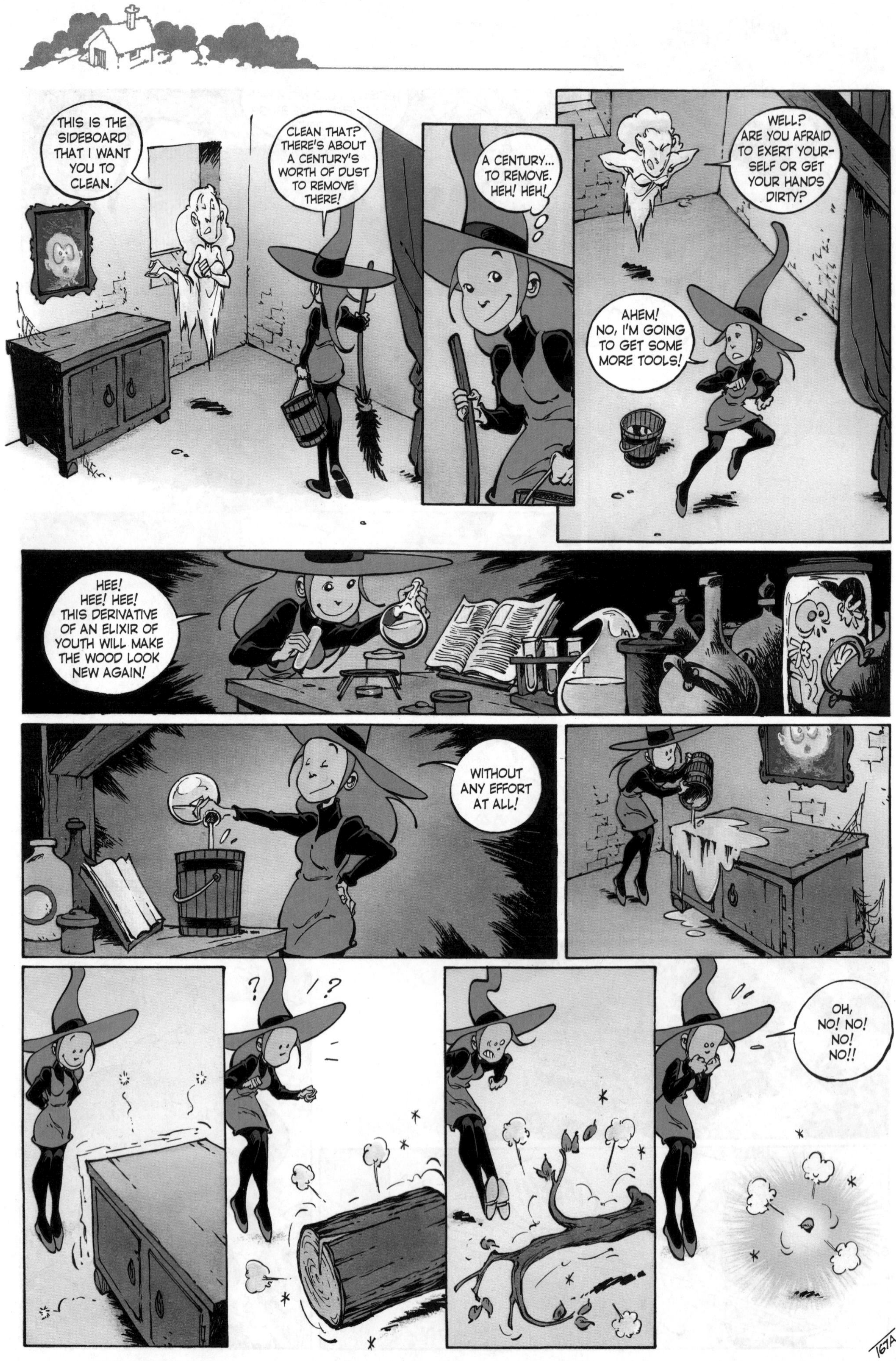
THIS IS THE SIDEBOARD THAT I WANT YOU TO CLEAN.
CLEAN THAT? THERE'S ABOUT A CENTURY'S WORTH OF DUST TO REMOVE THERE!
A CENTURY... TO REMOVE. HEH! HEH!
WELL? ARE YOU AFRAID TO EXERT YOUR-SELF OR GET YOUR HANDS DIRTY?
AHEM! NO, I'M GOING TO GET SOME MORE TOOLS!
HEE! HEE! HEE! THIS DERIVATIVE OF AN ELIXIR OF YOUTH WILL MAKE THE WOOD LOOK NEW AGAIN!
WITHOUT ANY EFFORT AT ALL!
?
!?
OH, NO! NO! NO! NO!!
TETA

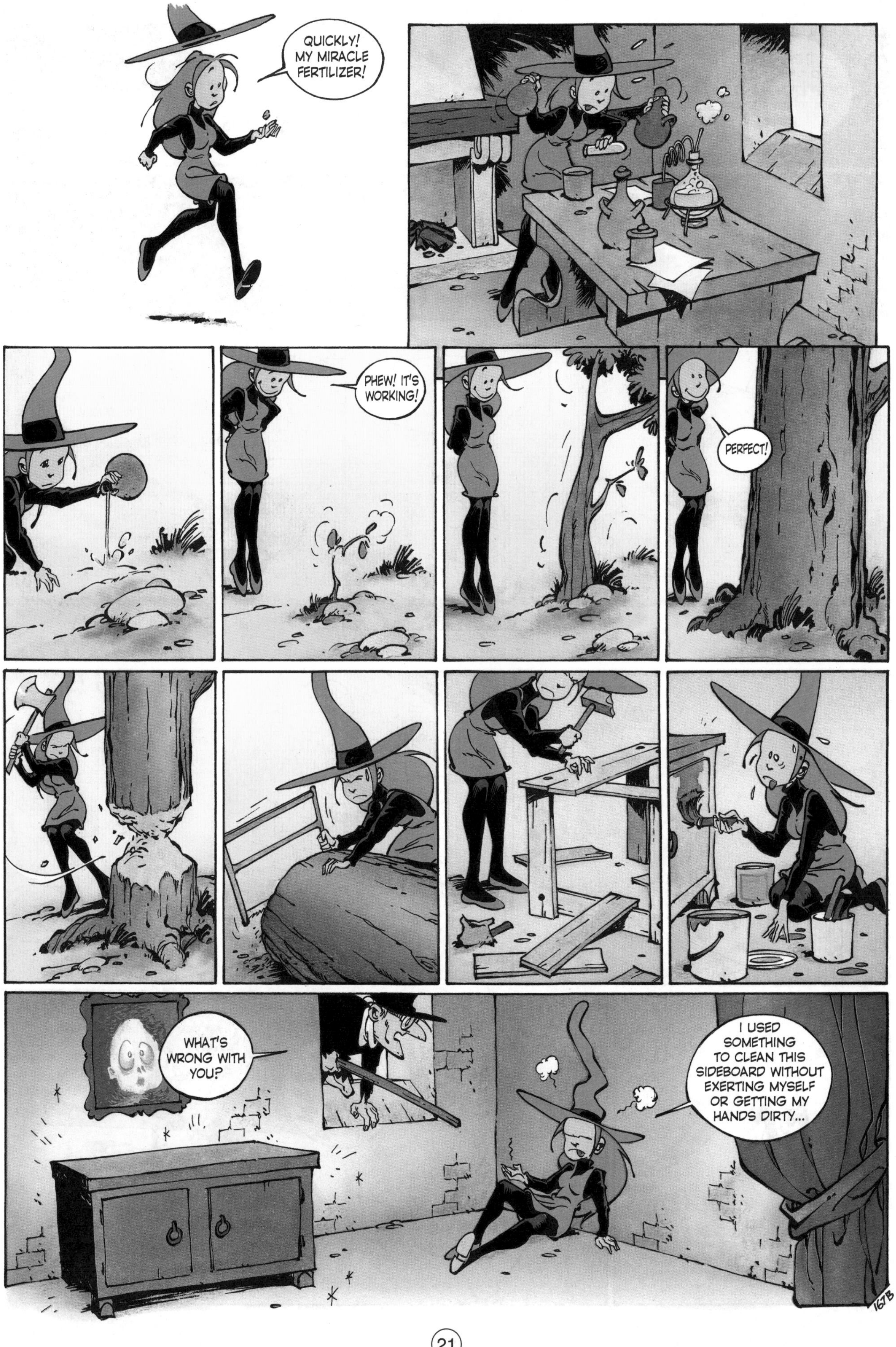
QUICKLY! MY MIRACLE FERTILIZER!
PHEW! IT'S WORKING!
PERFECT!
WHAT'S WRONG WITH YOU?
I USED SOMETHING TO CLEAN THIS SIDEBOARD WITHOUT EXERTING MYSELF OR GETTING MY HANDS DIRTY...

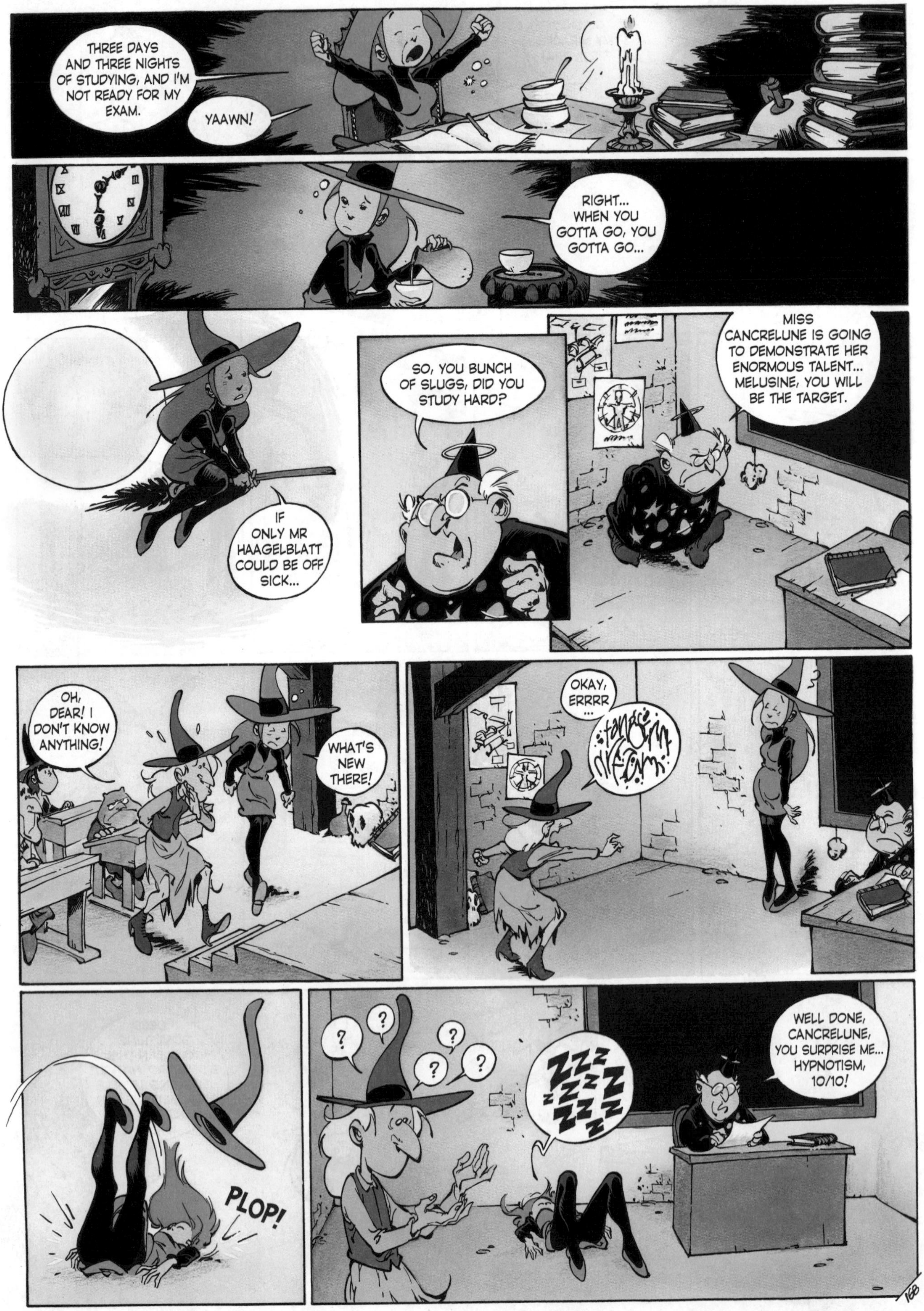
THREE DAYS AND THREE NIGHTS OF STUDYING, AND I'M NOT READY FOR MY EXAM.
YAAWN!
RIGHT... WHEN YOU GOTTA GO, YOU GOTTA GO...
IF ONLY MR HAAGELBLATT COULD BE OFF SICK...
SO, YOU BUNCH OF SLUGS, DID YOU STUDY HARD?
MISS CANCRELUNE IS GOING TO DEMONSTRATE HER ENORMOUS TALENT... MELUSINE, YOU WILL BE THE TARGET.
OH, DEAR! I DON'T KNOW ANYTHING!
WHAT'S NEW THERE!
OKAY, ERRRR ...
PLOP!
?
?
?
?
?
ZZZZZZZZZZ
WELL DONE, CANCRELUNE, YOU SURPRISE ME... HYPNOTISM, 10/10!

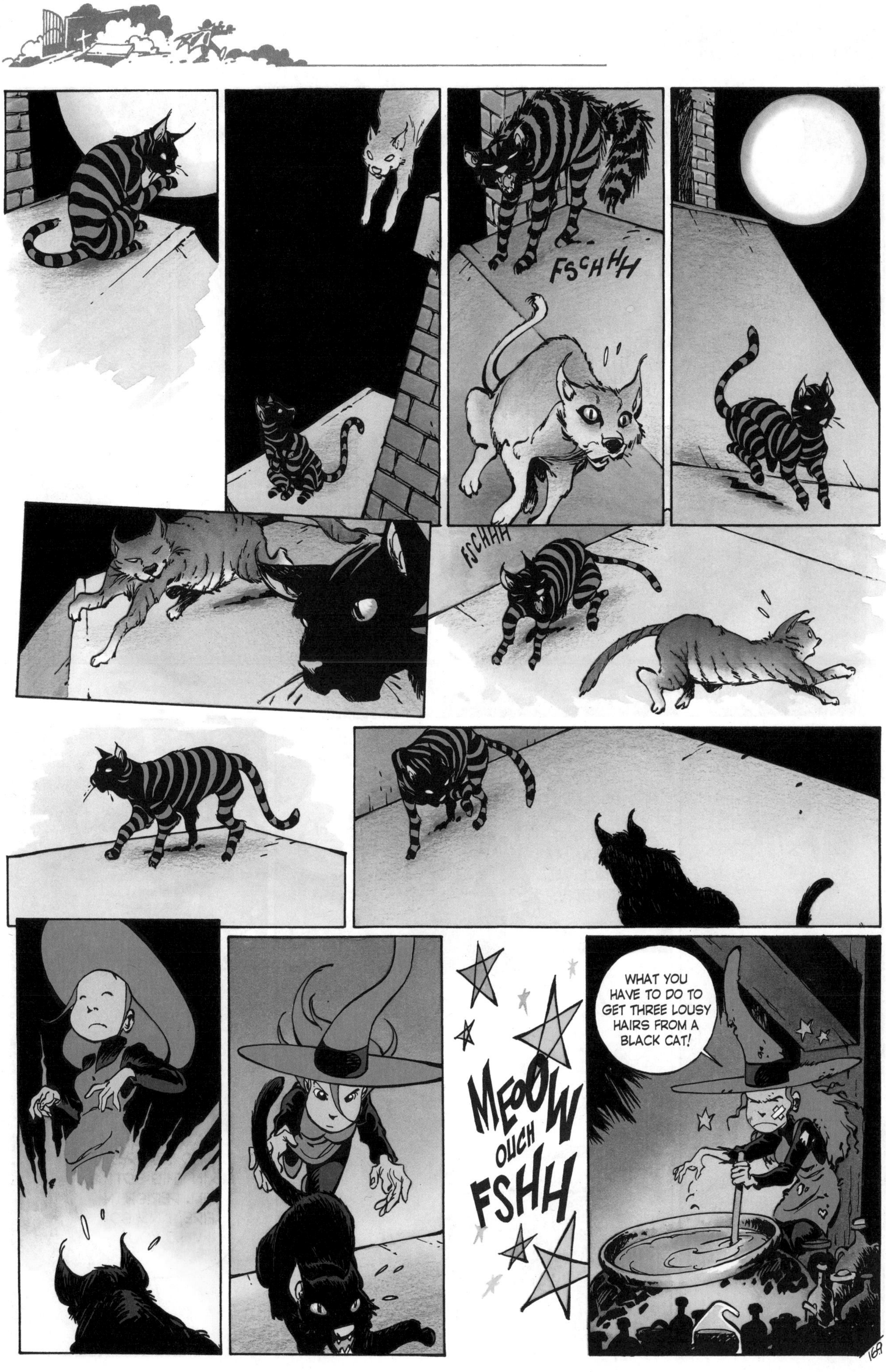
FSCHHH
FSCHHH
WHAT YOU HAVE TO DO TO GET THREE LOUSY HAIRS FROM A BLACK CAT!
MEOOW
OUCH
FSHH

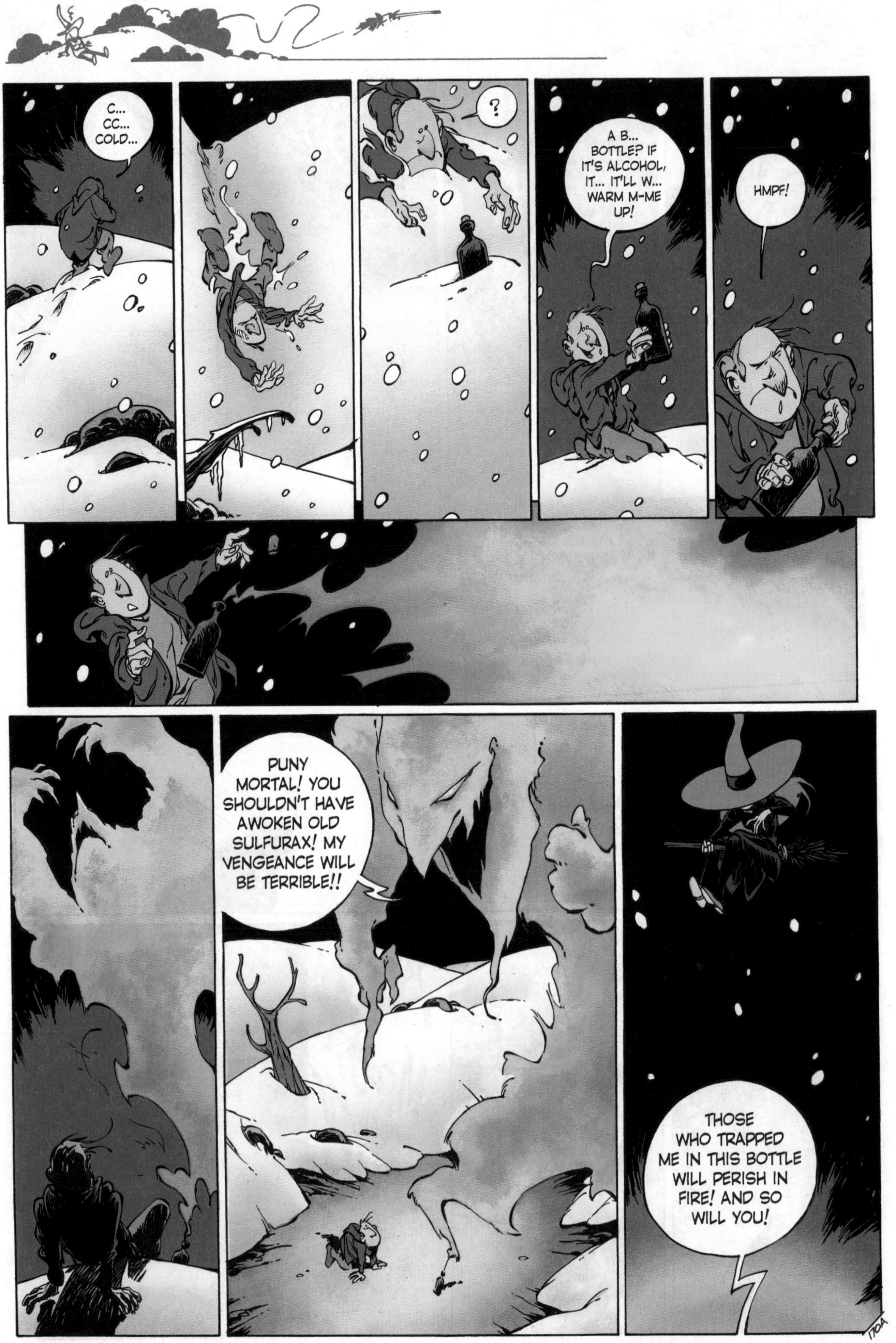
C... CC... COLD...
?
A B... BOTTLE? IF IT'S ALCOHOL, IT... IT'LL W... WARM M-ME UP!
HMPF!
PUNY MORTAL! YOU SHOULDN'T HAVE AWOKEN OLD SULFURAX! MY VENGEANCE WILL BE TERRIBLE!!
THOSE WHO TRAPPED ME IN THIS BOTTLE WILL PERISH IN FIRE! AND SO WILL YOU!

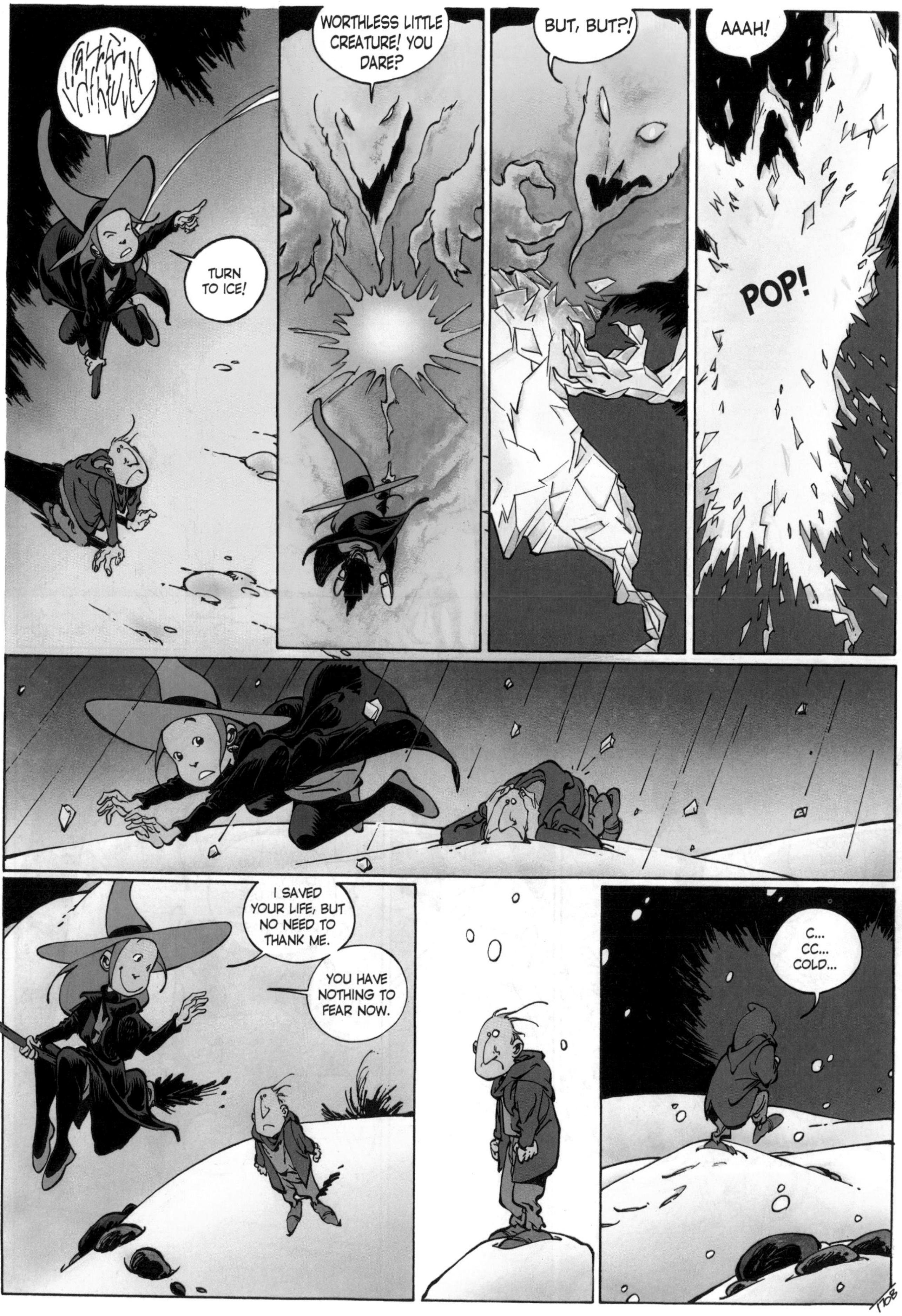
TURN TO ICE!
WORTHLESS LITTLE CREATURE! YOU DARE?
BUT, BUT?!
AAAH!
POP!
I SAVED YOUR LIFE, BUT NO NEED TO THANK ME.
YOU HAVE NOTHING TO FEAR NOW.
C... CC... COLD...

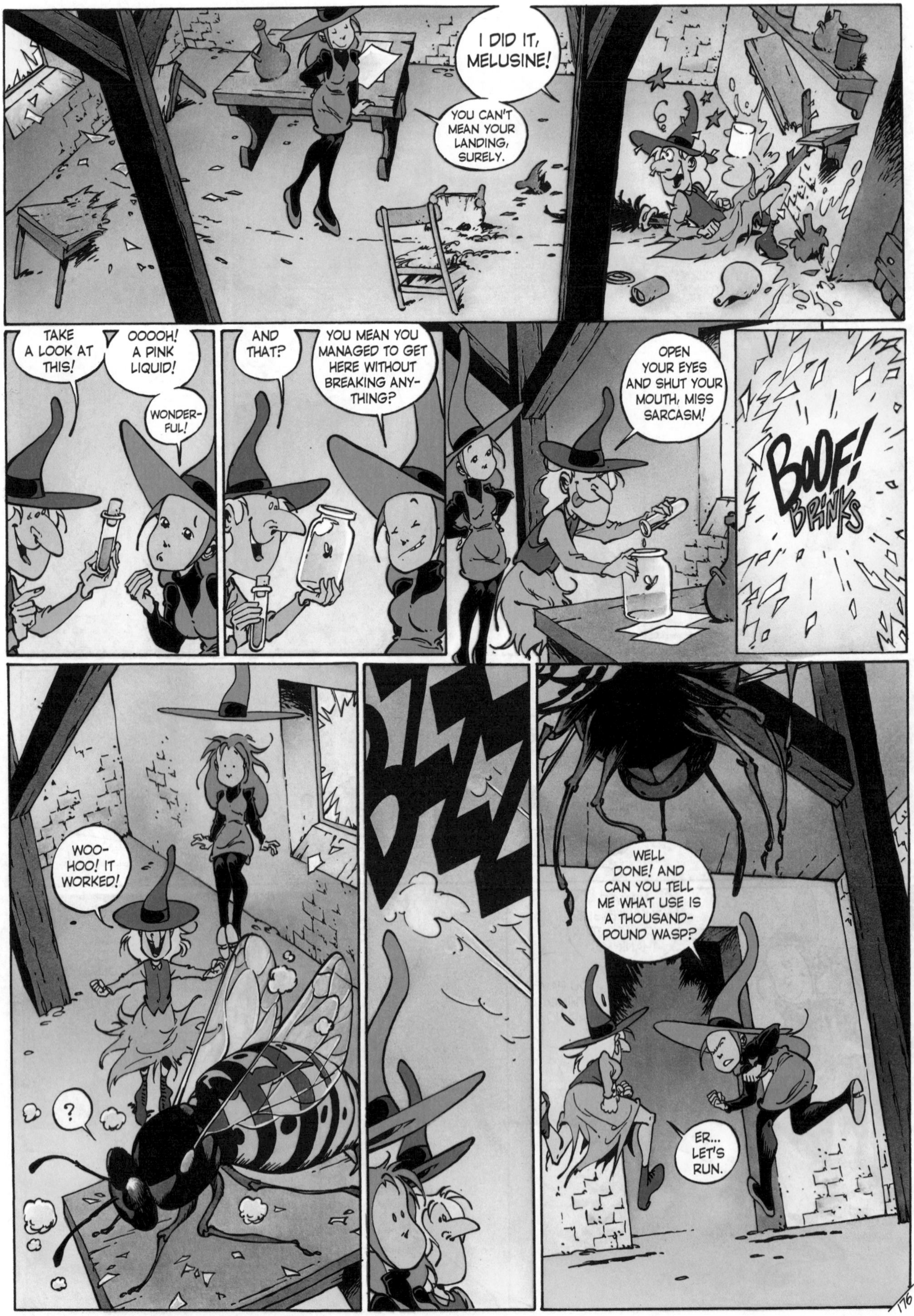
I DID IT, MELUSINE!
YOU CAN'T MEAN YOUR LANDING, SURELY.
TAKE A LOOK AT THIS!
OOOOH! A PINK LIQUID!
WONDER-FUL!
AND THAT?
YOU MEAN YOU MANAGED TO GET HERE WITHOUT BREAKING ANY-THING?
OPEN YOUR EYES AND SHUT YOUR MOUTH, MISS SARCASM!
BOOF!
BRINKS
WOO-HOO! IT WORKED!
?
WELL DONE! AND CAN YOU TELL ME WHAT USE IS A THOUSAND-POUND WASP?
ER... LET'S RUN.

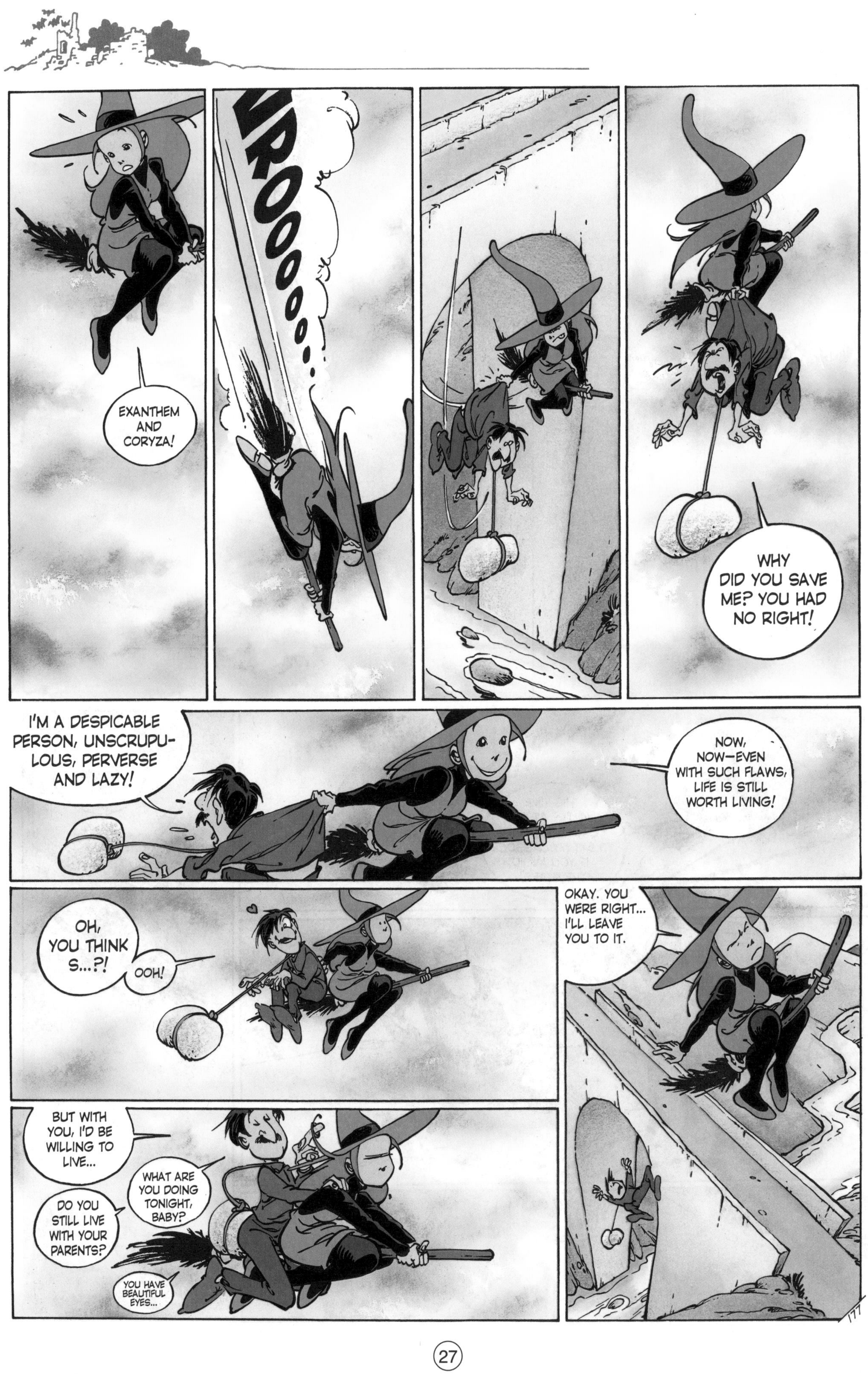
EXANTHEM AND CORYZA!
VROOOOOO...
WHY DID YOU SAVE ME? YOU HAD NO RIGHT!
I'M A DESPICABLE PERSON, UNSCRUPULOUS, PERVERSE AND LAZY!
NOW, NOW—EVEN WITH SUCH FLAWS, LIFE IS STILL WORTH LIVING!
OH, YOU THINK S...?!
OOH!
OKAY. YOU WERE RIGHT... I'LL LEAVE YOU TO IT.
BUT WITH YOU, I'D BE WILLING TO LIVE...
WHAT ARE YOU DOING TONIGHT, BABY?
DO YOU STILL LIVE WITH YOUR PARENTS?
YOU HAVE BEAUTIFUL EYES...

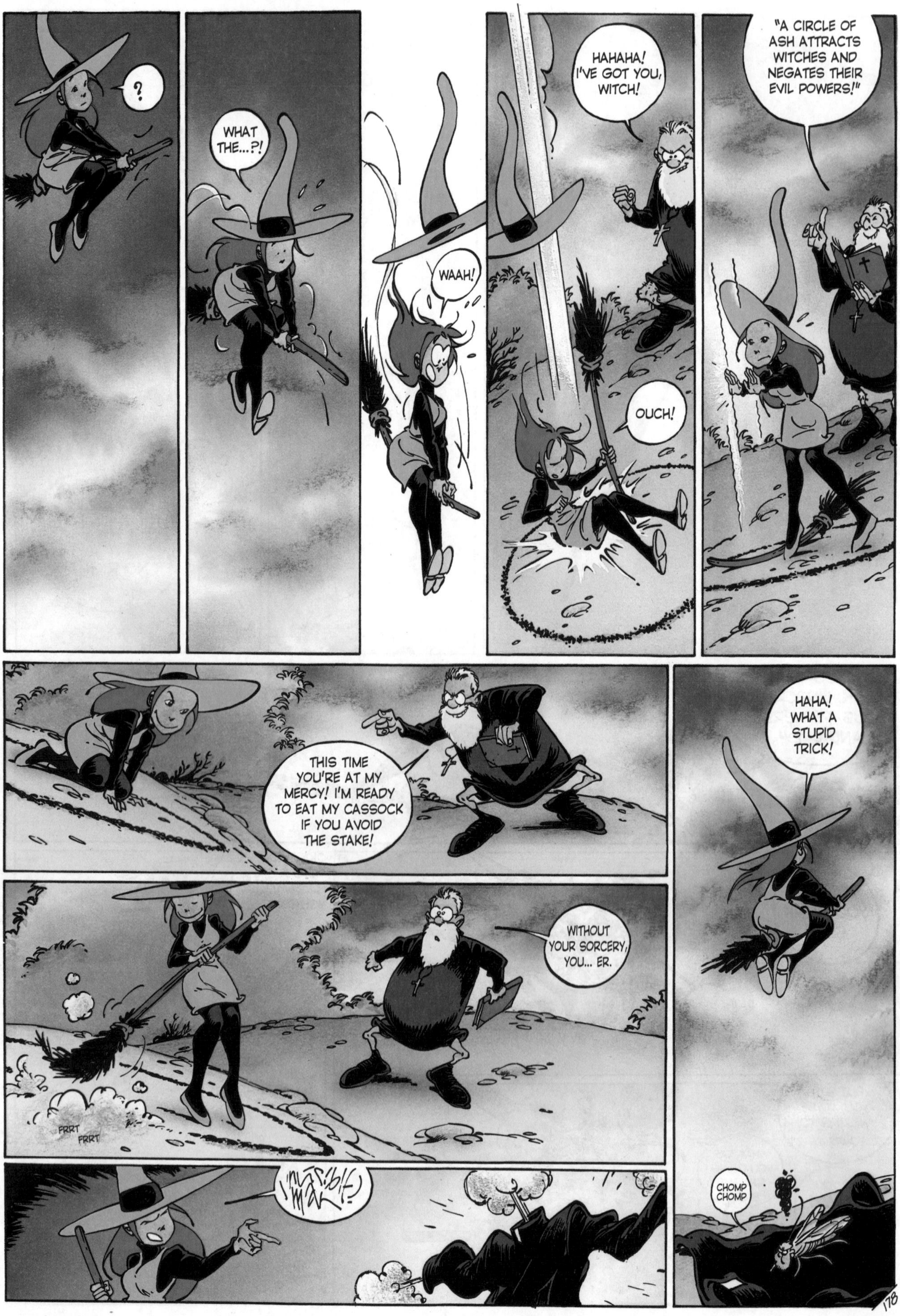
?
WHAT THE...?!
WAAH!
HAHAHA! I'VE GOT YOU, WITCH!
OUCH!
"A CIRCLE OF ASH ATTRACTS WITCHES AND NEGATES THEIR EVIL POWERS!"
THIS TIME YOU'RE AT MY MERCY! I'M READY TO EAT MY CASSOCK IF YOU AVOID THE STAKE!
HAHA! WHAT A STUPID TRICK!
WITHOUT YOUR SORCERY, YOU... ER.
FRRT FRRT
CHOMP CHOMP

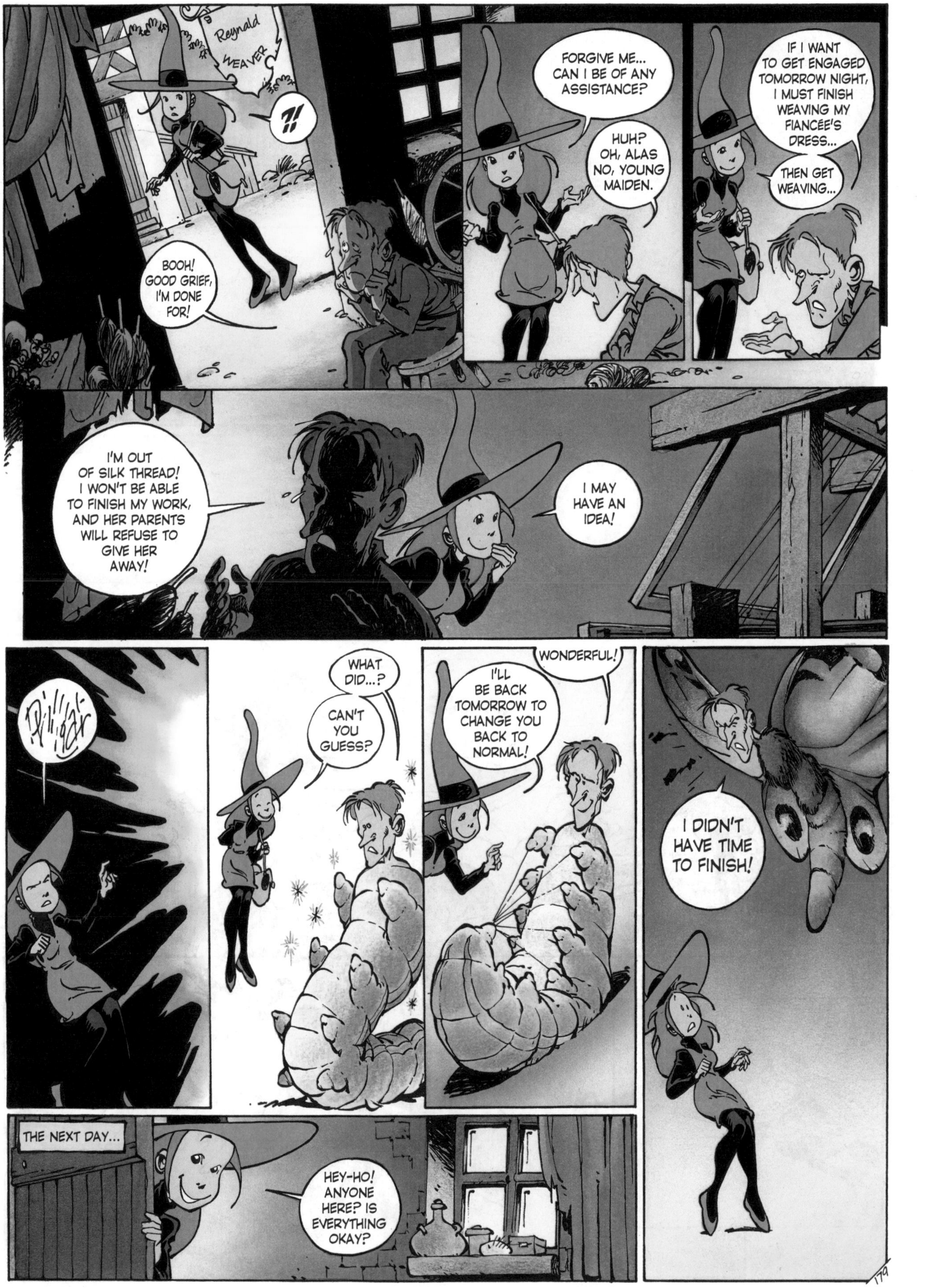
Reynald
WEAVER
?!
BOOH! GOOD GRIEF, I'M DONE FOR!
FORGIVE ME... CAN I BE OF ANY ASSISTANCE?
HUH? OH, ALAS NO, YOUNG MAIDEN.
IF I WANT TO GET ENGAGED TOMORROW NIGHT, I MUST FINISH WEAVING MY FIANCÉE'S DRESS...
THEN GET WEAVING...
I'M OUT OF SILK THREAD! I WON'T BE ABLE TO FINISH MY WORK, AND HER PARENTS WILL REFUSE TO GIVE HER AWAY!
I MAY HAVE AN IDEA!
WHAT DID...?
CAN'T YOU GUESS?
WONDERFUL!
I'LL BE BACK TOMORROW TO CHANGE YOU BACK TO NORMAL!
I DIDN'T HAVE TIME TO FINISH!
THE NEXT DAY...
HEY-HO! ANYONE HERE? IS EVERYTHING OKAY?

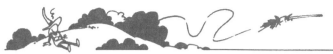

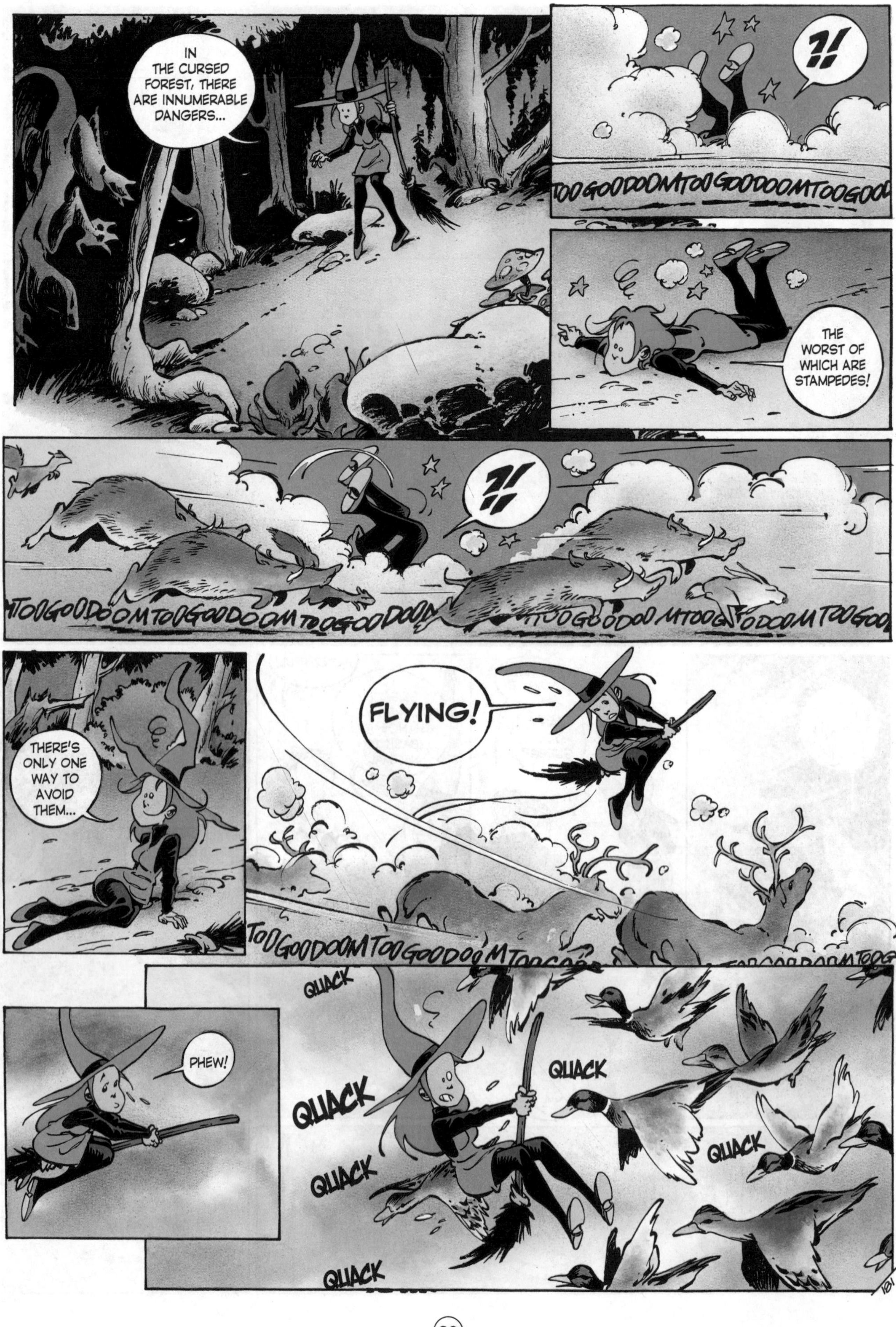
IN THE CURSED FOREST, THERE ARE INNUMERABLE DANGERS...
?!
TOOGOODOOMTOOGOODOOMTOOGOO
THE WORST OF WHICH ARE STAMPEDES!
?!
TOOGOODOOMTOOGOODOOMTOOGOODOOM
THERE'S ONLY ONE WAY TO AVOID THEM...
FLYING!
TOOGOODOOMTOOGOODOOM
QUACK
PHEW!
QUACK
QUACK
QUACK
QUACK
QUACK

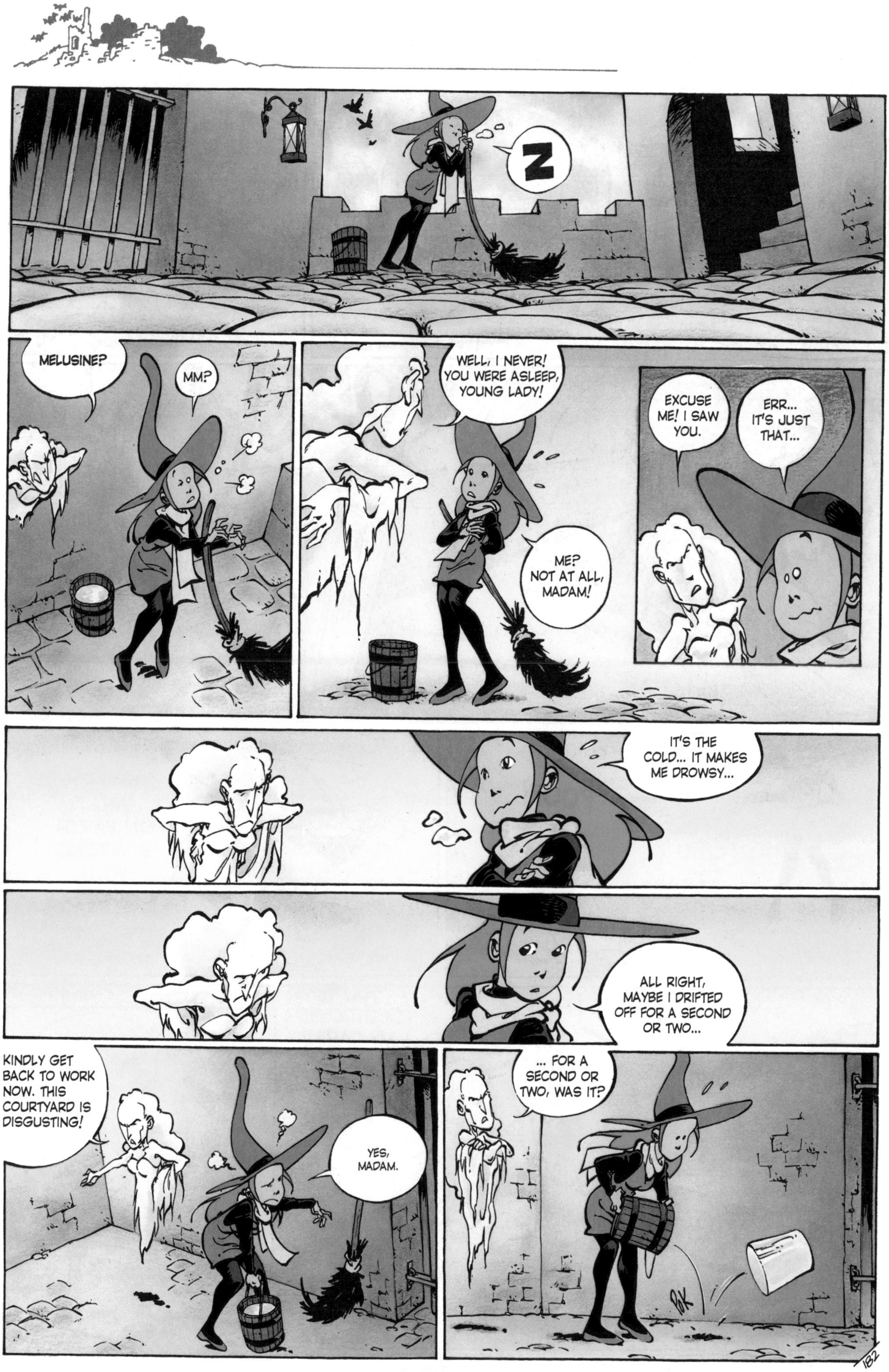

Z
MELUSINE?
MM?
WELL, I NEVER! YOU WERE ASLEEP, YOUNG LADY!
ME? NOT AT ALL, MADAM!
EXCUSE ME! I SAW YOU.
ERR... IT'S JUST THAT...
IT'S THE COLD... IT MAKES ME DROWSY...
ALL RIGHT, MAYBE I DRIFTED OFF FOR A SECOND OR TWO...
KINDLY GET BACK TO WORK NOW. THIS COURTYARD IS DISGUSTING!
YES, MADAM.
... FOR A SECOND OR TWO, WAS IT?
POK

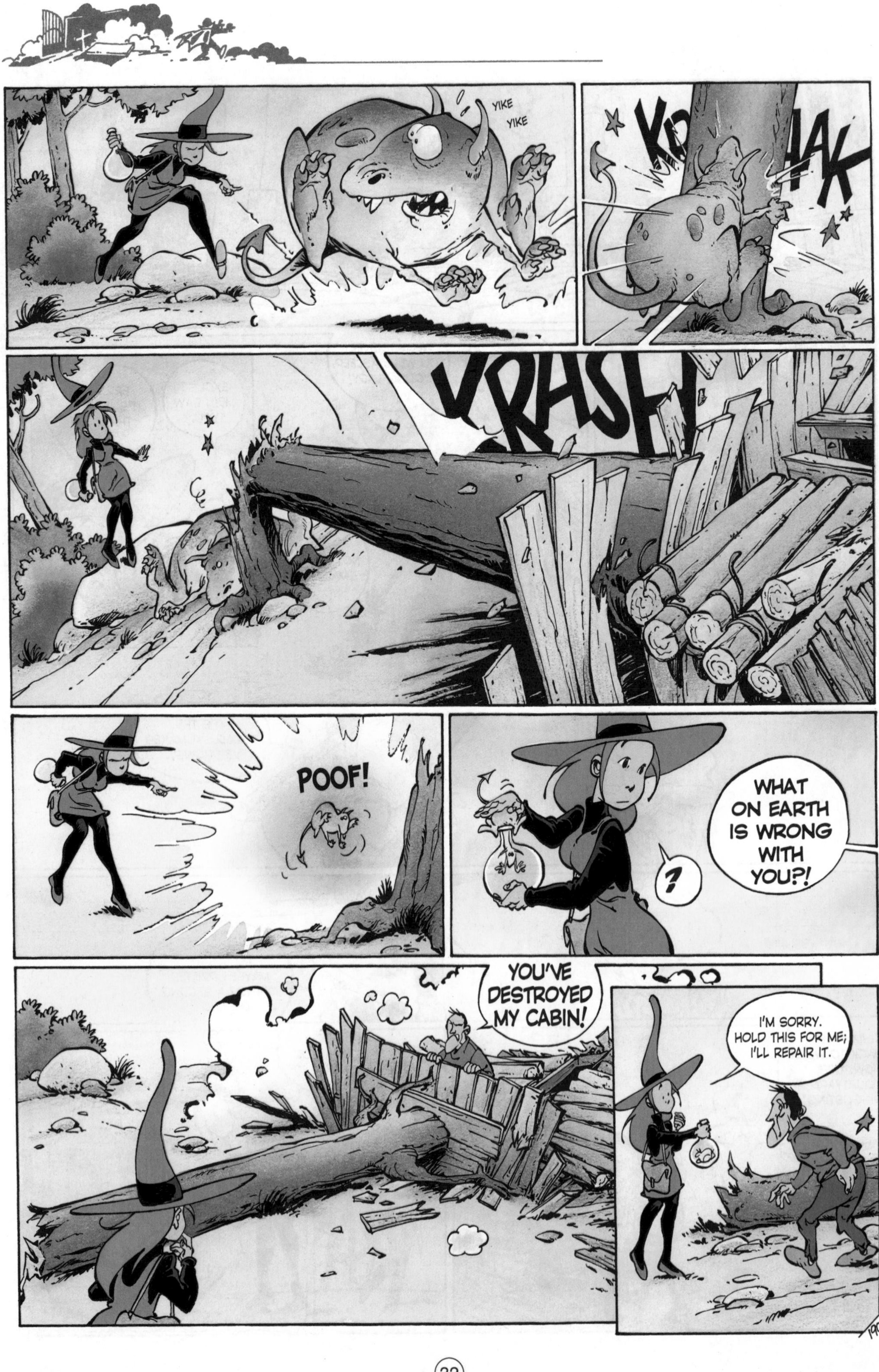
YIKE
YIKE
KO...AK
KRASH
POOF!
?
WHAT ON EARTH IS WRONG WITH YOU?!
YOU'VE DESTROYED MY CABIN!
I'M SORRY. HOLD THIS FOR ME; I'LL REPAIR IT.

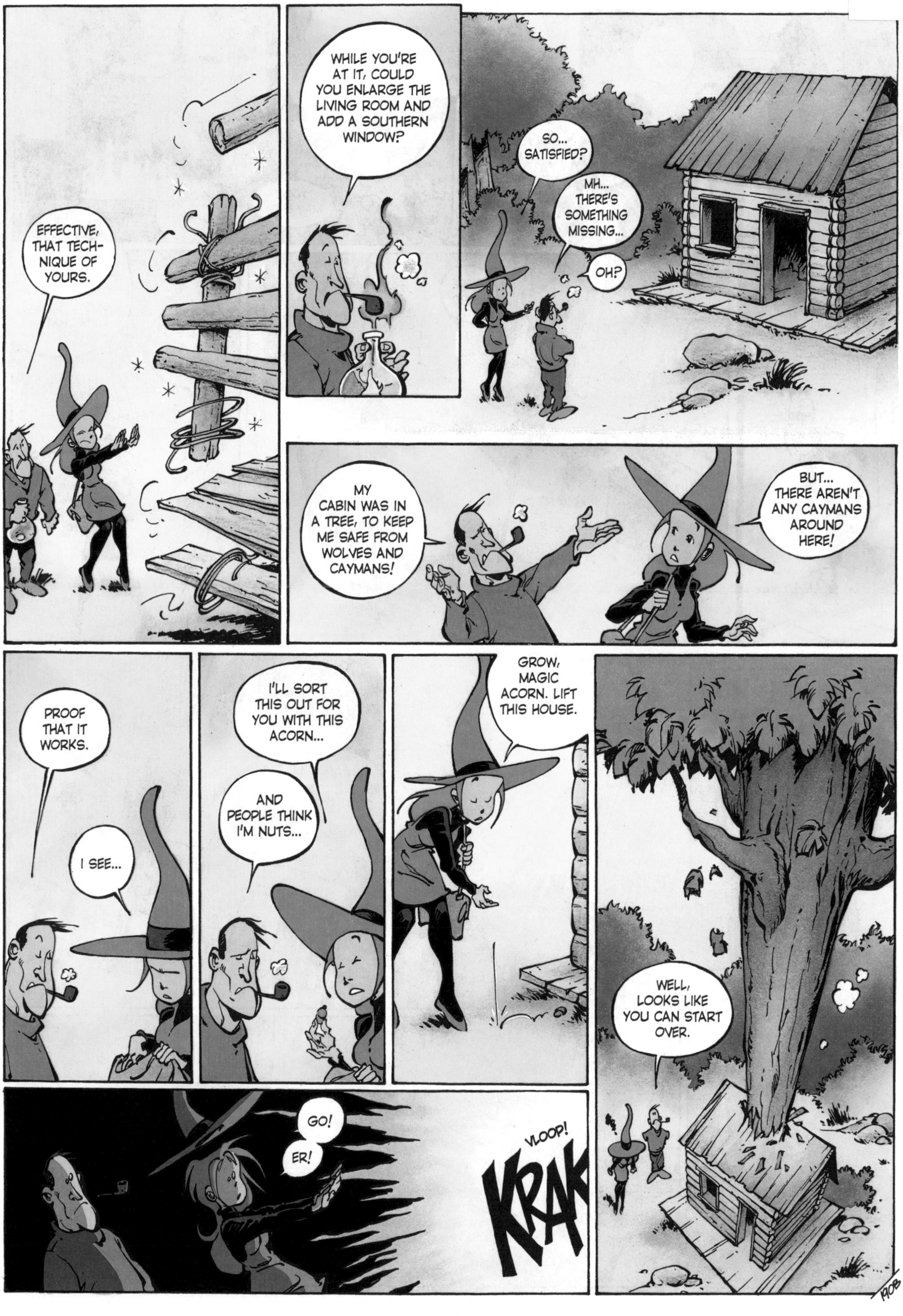
EFFECTIVE, THAT TECHNIQUE OF YOURS.
WHILE YOU'RE AT IT, COULD YOU ENLARGE THE LIVING ROOM AND ADD A SOUTHERN WINDOW?
SO... SATISFIED?
MH... THERE'S SOMETHING MISSING...
OH?
MY CABIN WAS IN A TREE, TO KEEP ME SAFE FROM WOLVES AND CAYMANS!
BUT... THERE AREN'T ANY CAYMANS AROUND HERE!
PROOF THAT IT WORKS.
I SEE...
I'LL SORT THIS OUT FOR YOU WITH THIS ACORN...
AND PEOPLE THINK I'M NUTS...
GROW, MAGIC ACORN. LIFT THIS HOUSE.
GO!
ER!
VLOOP!
KRAK
WELL, LOOKS LIKE YOU CAN START OVER.

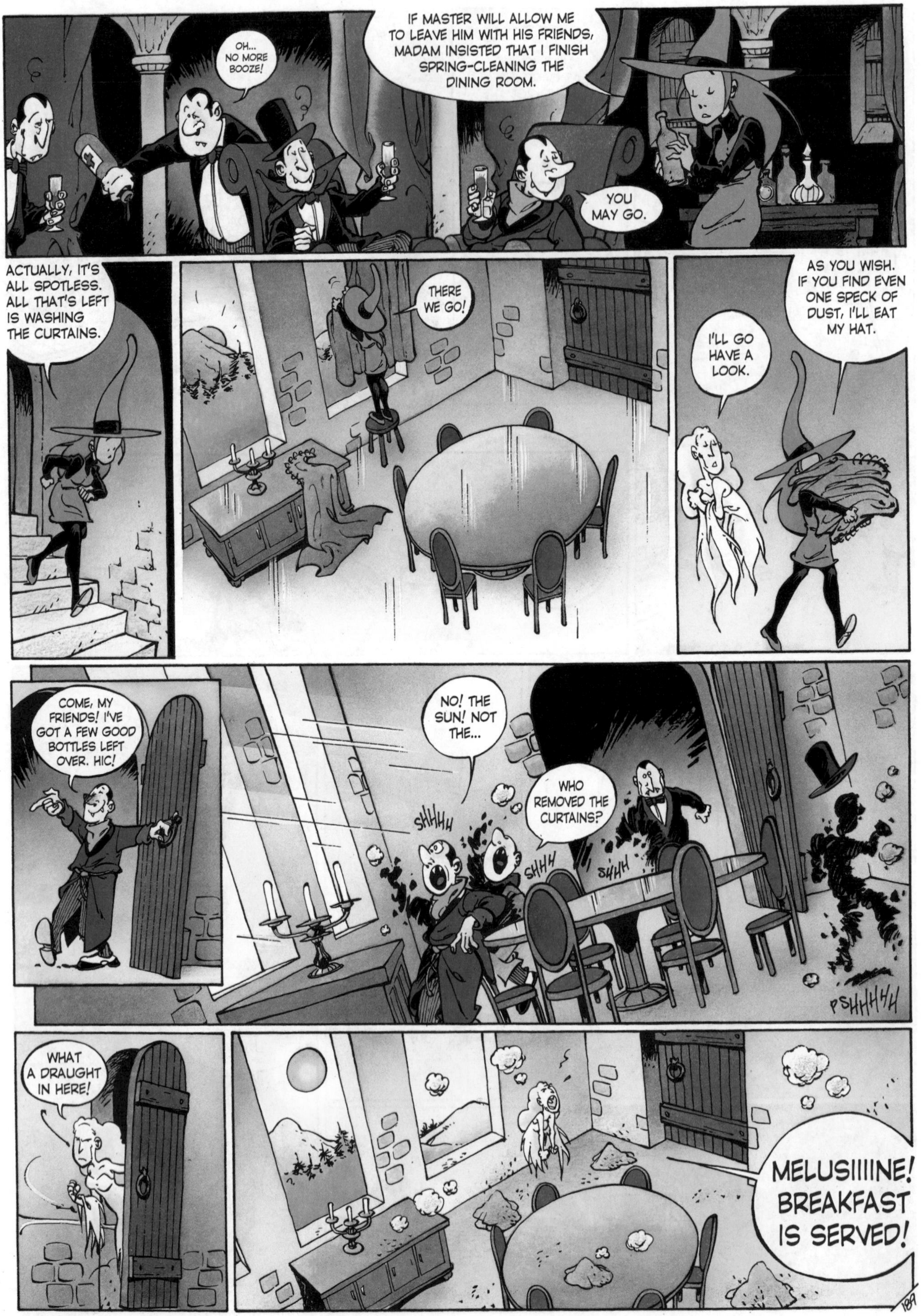
OH... NO MORE BOOZE!
IF MASTER WILL ALLOW ME TO LEAVE HIM WITH HIS FRIENDS, MADAM INSISTED THAT I FINISH SPRING-CLEANING THE DINING ROOM.
YOU MAY GO.
ACTUALLY, IT'S ALL SPOTLESS. ALL THAT'S LEFT IS WASHING THE CURTAINS.
THERE WE GO!
AS YOU WISH. IF YOU FIND EVEN ONE SPECK OF DUST, I'LL EAT MY HAT.
I'LL GO HAVE A LOOK.
COME, MY FRIENDS! I'VE GOT A FEW GOOD BOTTLES LEFT OVER. HIC!
NO! THE SUN! NOT THE...
WHO REMOVED THE CURTAINS?
SHHHH
SHHH
SHHH
PSHHHHH
WHAT A DRAUGHT IN HERE!
MELUSIIIINE! BREAKFAST IS SERVED!

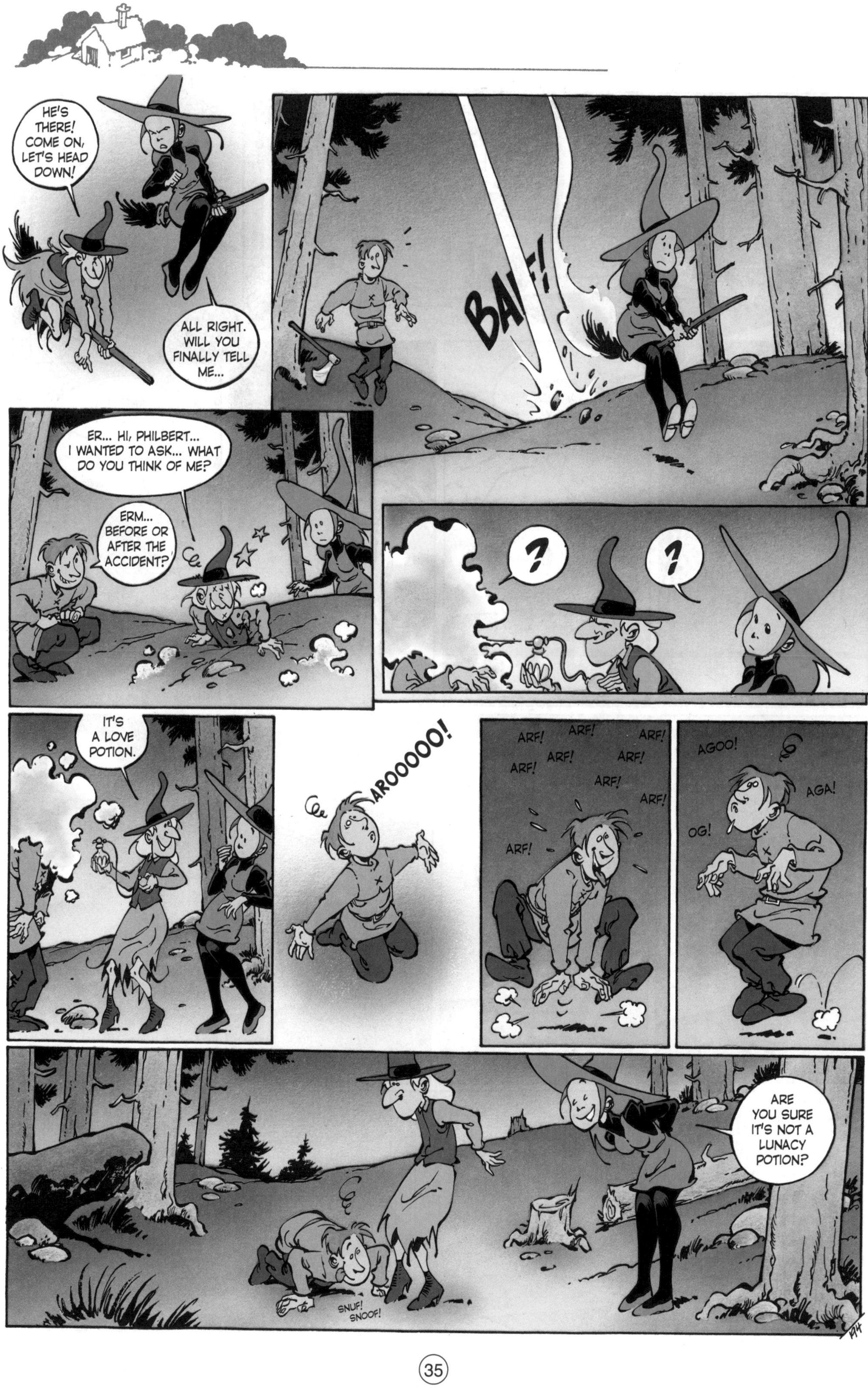

HE'S THERE! COME ON, LET'S HEAD DOWN!
ALL RIGHT. WILL YOU FINALLY TELL ME...
BAF!
ER... HI, PHILBERT... I WANTED TO ASK... WHAT DO YOU THINK OF ME?
ERM... BEFORE OR AFTER THE ACCIDENT?
?
?
IT'S A LOVE POTION.
AROOOOO!
ARF! ARF! ARF! ARF! ARF! ARF! ARF! ARF! ARF!
AGOO!
AGA!
OG!
SNUF! SNOOF!
ARE YOU SURE IT'S NOT A LUNACY POTION?

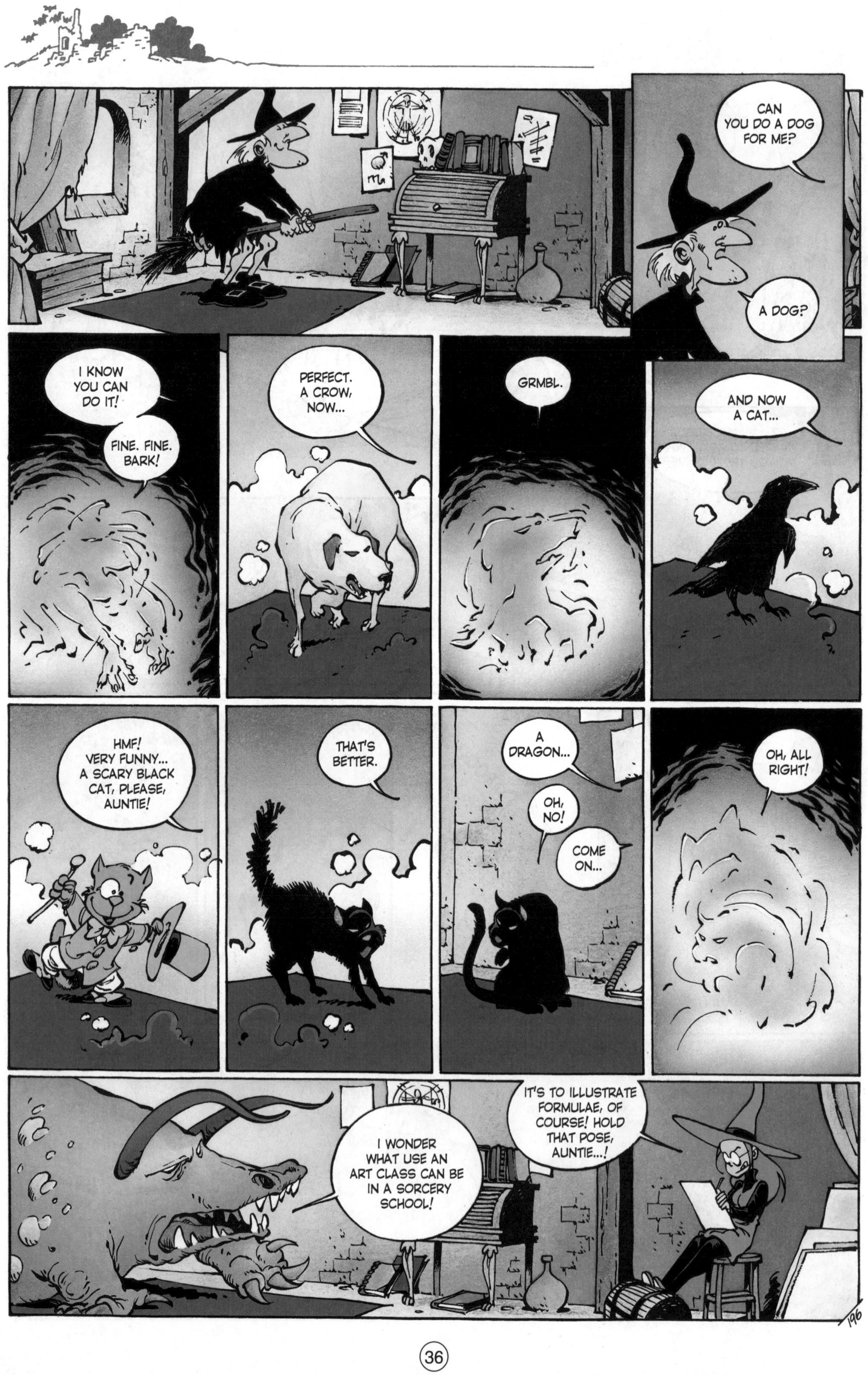

CAN YOU DO A DOG FOR ME?
A DOG?
I KNOW YOU CAN DO IT!
FINE. FINE. BARK!
PERFECT. A CROW, NOW...
GRMBL.
AND NOW A CAT...
HMF! VERY FUNNY... A SCARY BLACK CAT, PLEASE, AUNTIE!
THAT'S BETTER.
A DRAGON...
OH, NO!
COME ON...
OH, ALL RIGHT!
I WONDER WHAT USE AN ART CLASS CAN BE IN A SORCERY SCHOOL!
IT'S TO ILLUSTRATE FORMULAE, OF COURSE! HOLD THAT POSE, AUNTIE...!
196

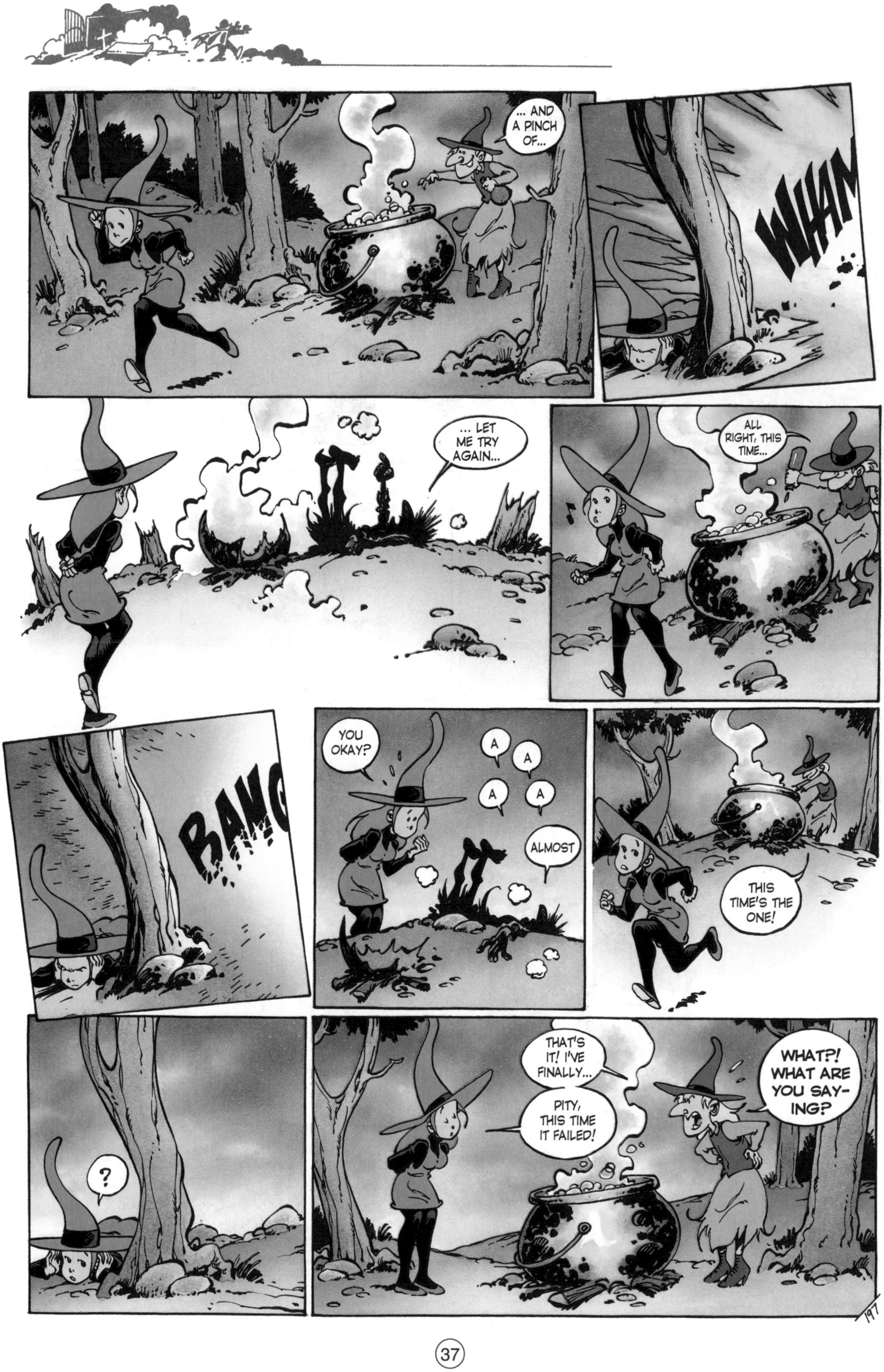
... AND A PINCH OF...
WHAM
... LET ME TRY AGAIN...
ALL RIGHT, THIS TIME...
BANG
YOU OKAY?
A
A
A
A
ALMOST
THIS TIME'S THE ONE!
?
THAT'S IT! I'VE FINALLY...
PITY, THIS TIME IT FAILED!
WHAT?! WHAT ARE YOU SAY-ING?

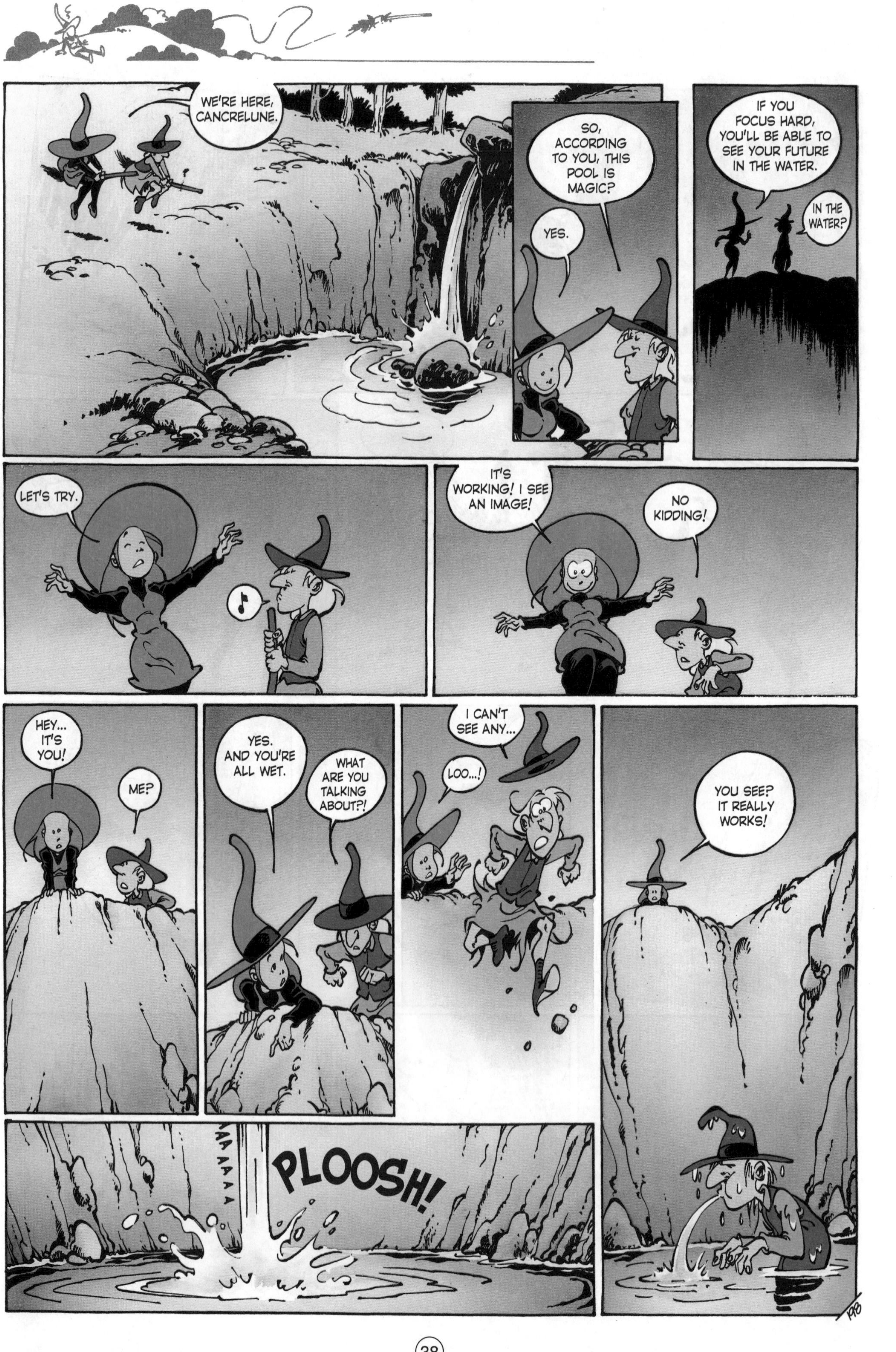
WE'RE HERE, CANCRELUNE.
SO, ACCORDING TO YOU, THIS POOL IS MAGIC?
YES.
IF YOU FOCUS HARD, YOU'LL BE ABLE TO SEE YOUR FUTURE IN THE WATER.
IN THE WATER?
LET'S TRY.
IT'S WORKING! I SEE AN IMAGE!
NO KIDDING!
HEY... IT'S YOU!
ME?
YES. AND YOU'RE ALL WET.
WHAT ARE YOU TALKING ABOUT?!
I CAN'T SEE ANY...
LOO...!
YOU SEE? IT REALLY WORKS!
AAAAAAA
PLOOSH!

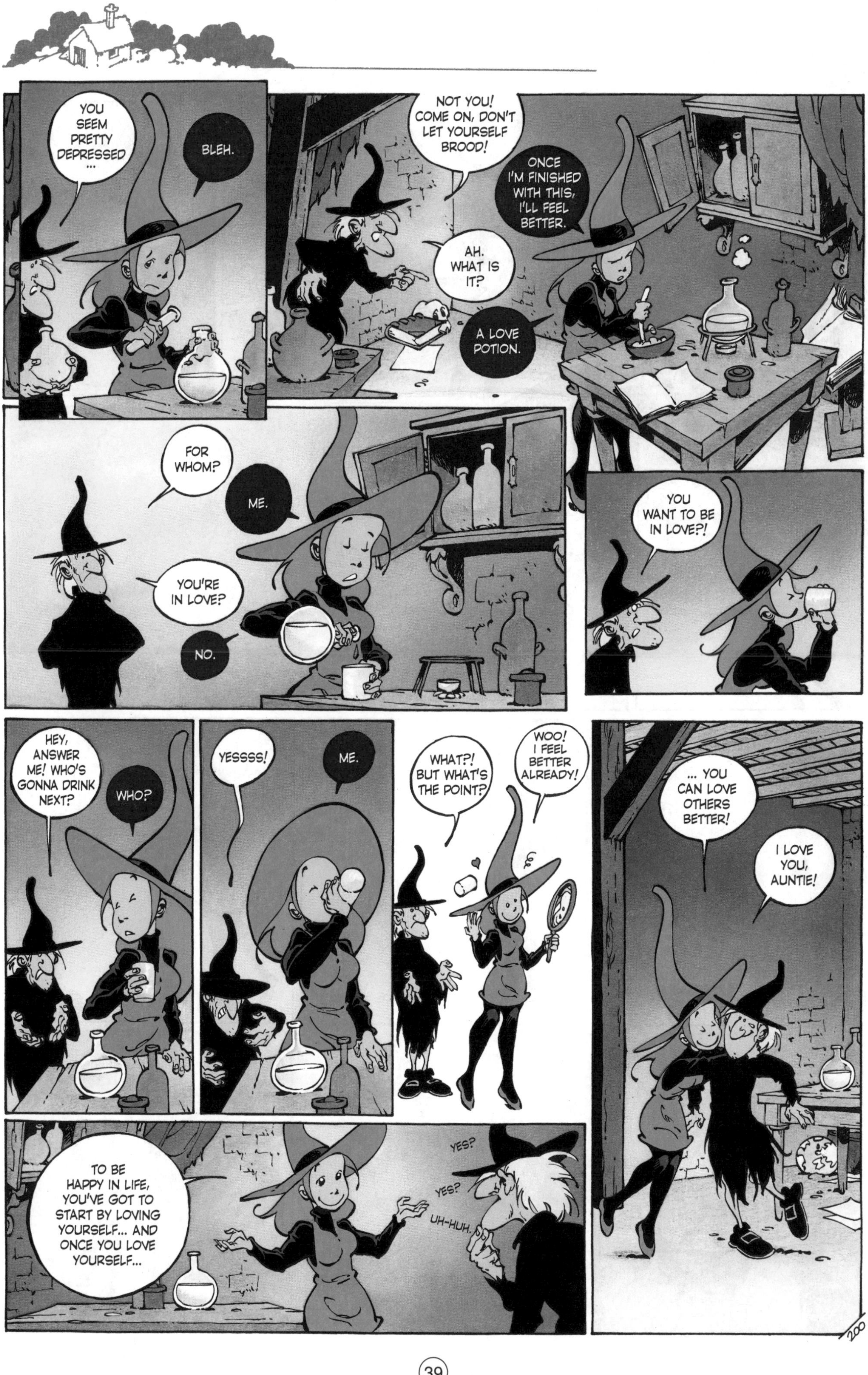

YOU SEEM PRETTY DEPRESSED ...
BLEH.
NOT YOU! COME ON, DON'T LET YOURSELF BROOD!
ONCE I'M FINISHED WITH THIS, I'LL FEEL BETTER.
AH. WHAT IS IT?
A LOVE POTION.
FOR WHOM?
ME.
YOU'RE IN LOVE?
NO.
YOU WANT TO BE IN LOVE?!
HEY, ANSWER ME! WHO'S GONNA DRINK NEXT?
WHO?
YESSSS!
ME.
WHAT?! BUT WHAT'S THE POINT?
WOO! I FEEL BETTER ALREADY!
TO BE HAPPY IN LIFE, YOU'VE GOT TO START BY LOVING YOURSELF... AND ONCE YOU LOVE YOURSELF...
YES?
YES?
UH-HUH.
... YOU CAN LOVE OTHERS BETTER!
I LOVE YOU, AUNTIE!
200

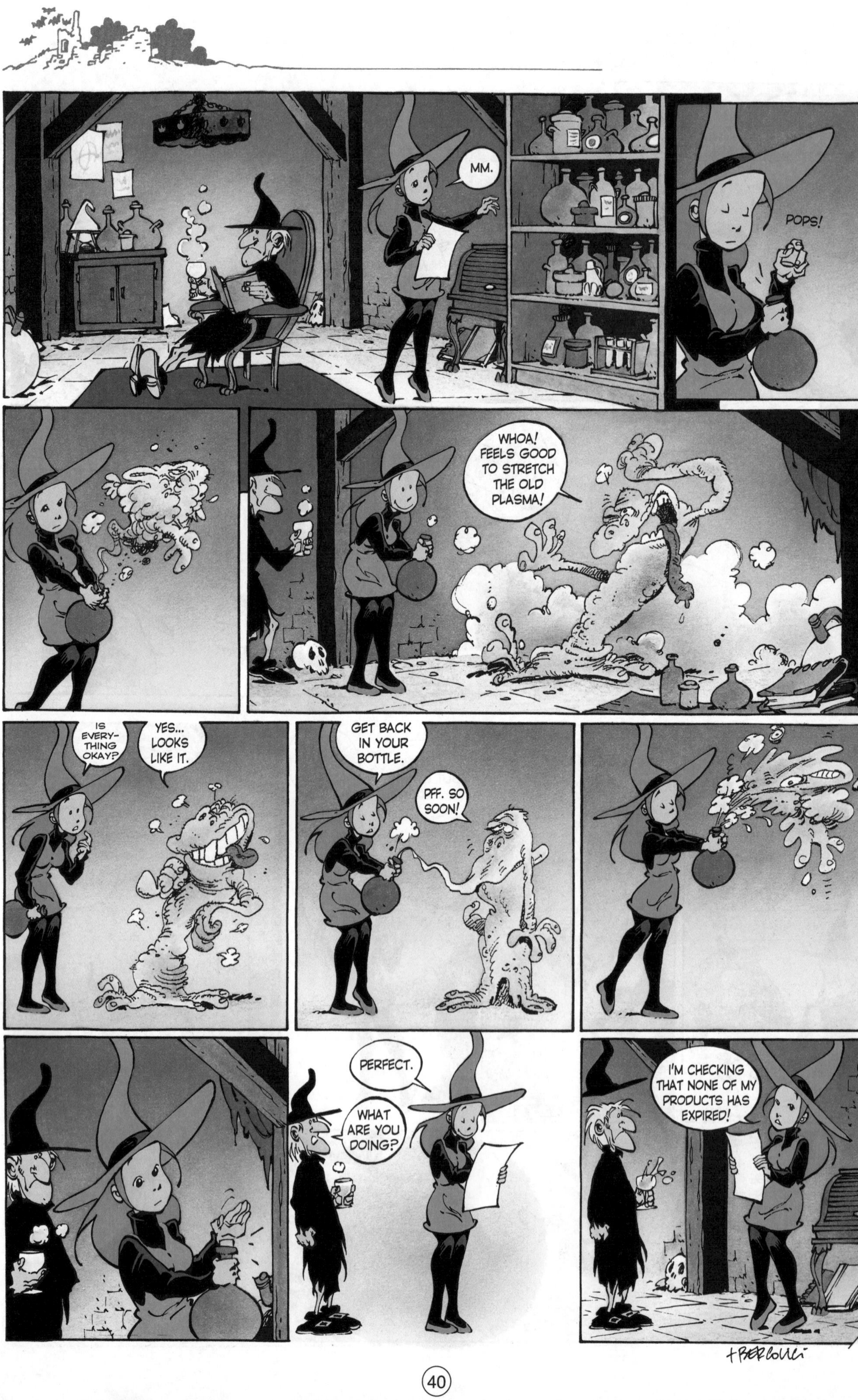
MM.
POPS!
WHOA! FEELS GOOD TO STRETCH THE OLD PLASMA!
IS EVERY-THING OKAY?
YES... LOOKS LIKE IT.
GET BACK IN YOUR BOTTLE.
PFF. SO SOON!
PERFECT.
WHAT ARE YOU DOING?
I'M CHECKING THAT NONE OF MY PRODUCTS HAS EXPIRED!
201
T BERCOVICI

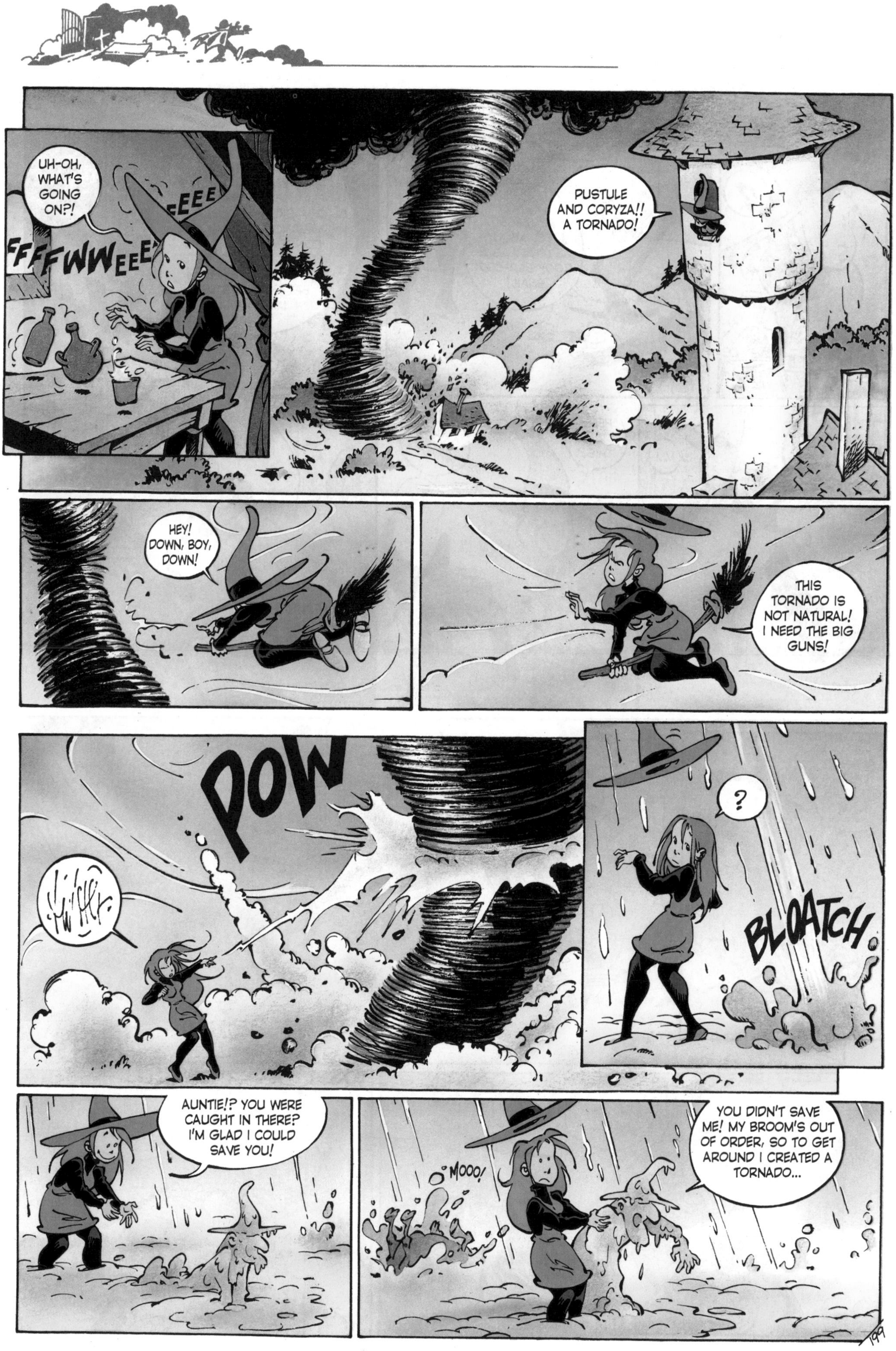
UH-OH, WHAT'S GOING ON?!
FFFFWWEEEEEEEE
PUSTULE AND CORYZA!! A TORNADO!
HEY! DOWN, BOY, DOWN!
THIS TORNADO IS NOT NATURAL! I NEED THE BIG GUNS!
POW
?
BLOATCH
AUNTIE!? YOU WERE CAUGHT IN THERE? I'M GLAD I COULD SAVE YOU!
MOOO!
YOU DIDN'T SAVE ME! MY BROOM'S OUT OF ORDER, SO TO GET AROUND I CREATED A TORNADO...

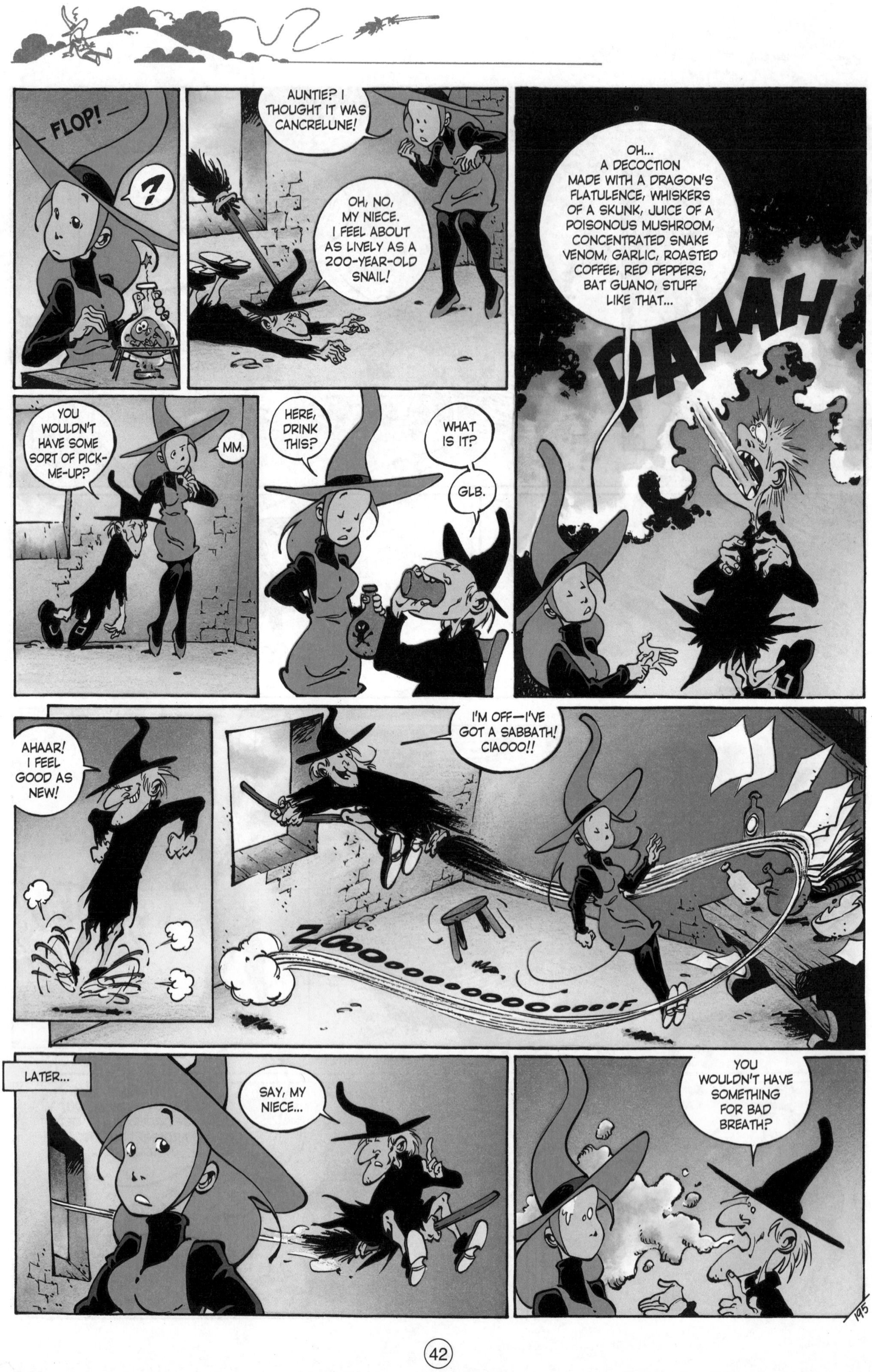
FLOP!
?
AUNTIE? I THOUGHT IT WAS CANCRELUNE!
OH, NO, MY NIECE. I FEEL ABOUT AS LIVELY AS A 200-YEAR-OLD SNAIL!
OH... A DECOCTION MADE WITH A DRAGON'S FLATULENCE, WHISKERS OF A SKUNK, JUICE OF A POISONOUS MUSHROOM, CONCENTRATED SNAKE VENOM, GARLIC, ROASTED COFFEE, RED PEPPERS, BAT GUANO, STUFF LIKE THAT...
RAAAH
YOU WOULDN'T HAVE SOME SORT OF PICK-ME-UP?
MM.
HERE, DRINK THIS?
WHAT IS IT?
GLB.
AHAAR! I FEEL GOOD AS NEW!
I'M OFF—I'VE GOT A SABBATH! CIAOOO!!
ZOOOoooooooooooooooooF
LATER...
SAY, MY NIECE...
YOU WOULDN'T HAVE SOMETHING FOR BAD BREATH?
195

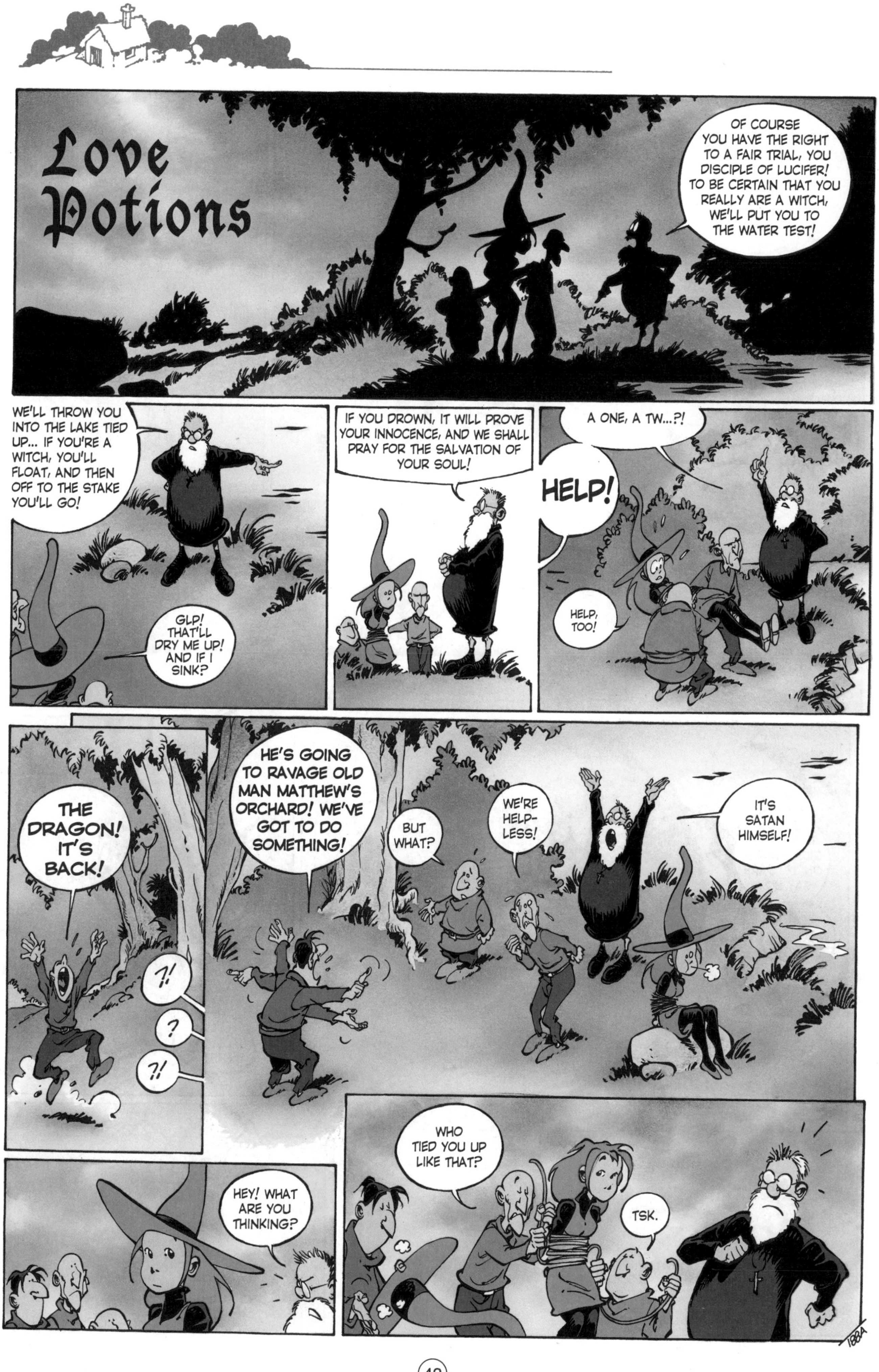
Love Potions
OF COURSE YOU HAVE THE RIGHT TO A FAIR TRIAL, YOU DISCIPLE OF LUCIFER! TO BE CERTAIN THAT YOU REALLY ARE A WITCH, WE'LL PUT YOU TO THE WATER TEST!
WE'LL THROW YOU INTO THE LAKE TIED UP... IF YOU'RE A WITCH, YOU'LL FLOAT, AND THEN OFF TO THE STAKE YOU'LL GO!
GLP! THAT'LL DRY ME UP! AND IF I SINK?
IF YOU DROWN, IT WILL PROVE YOUR INNOCENCE, AND WE SHALL PRAY FOR THE SALVATION OF YOUR SOUL!
A ONE, A TW...?!
HELP!
HELP, TOO!
THE DRAGON! IT'S BACK!
?!
?
?!
HE'S GOING TO RAVAGE OLD MAN MATTHEW'S ORCHARD! WE'VE GOT TO DO SOMETHING!
BUT WHAT?
WE'RE HELP-LESS!
IT'S SATAN HIMSELF!
HEY! WHAT ARE YOU THINKING?
WHO TIED YOU UP LIKE THAT?
TSK.
TIBBA

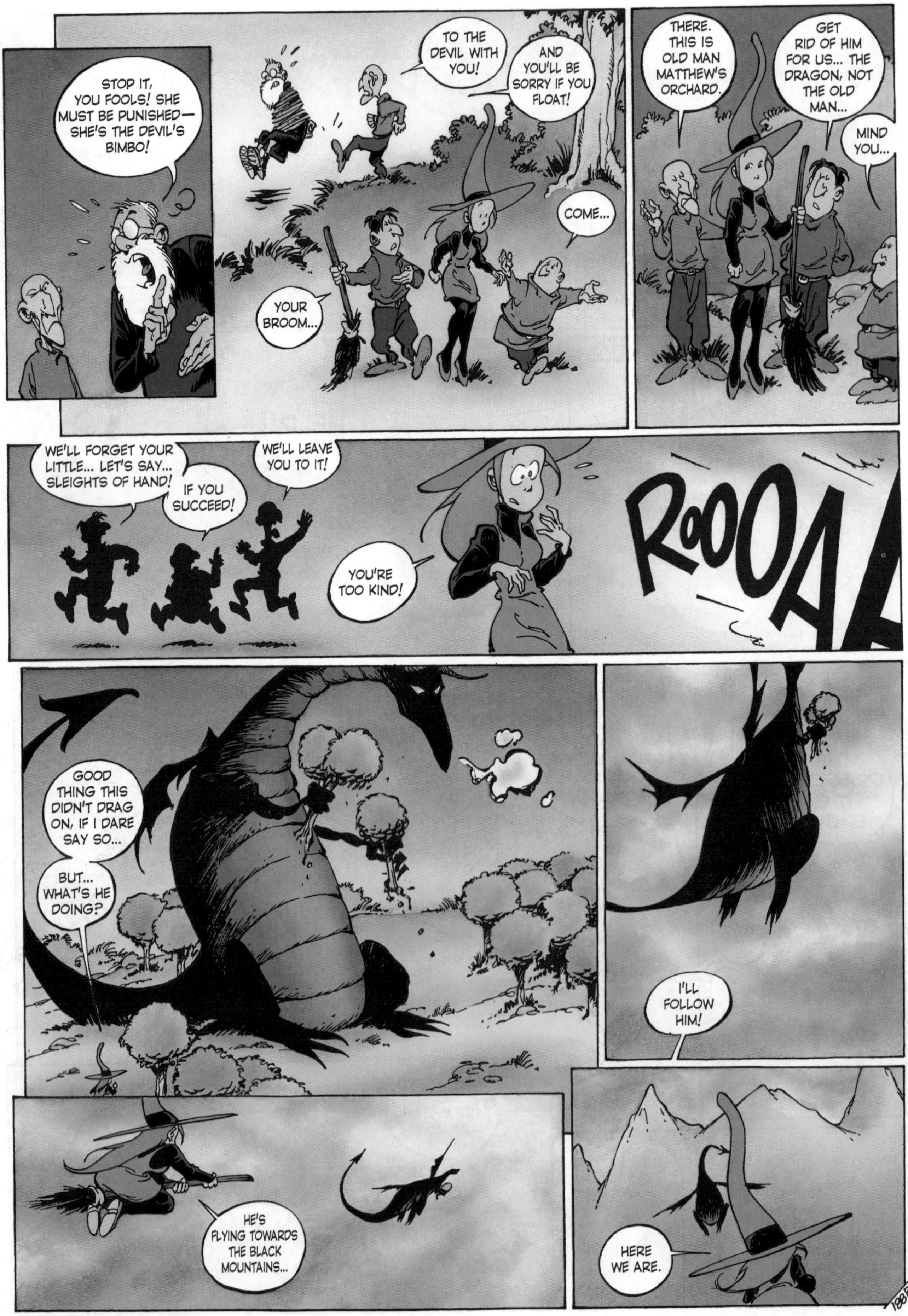

STOP IT, YOU FOOLS! SHE MUST BE PUNISHED— SHE'S THE DEVIL'S BIMBO!
TO THE DEVIL WITH YOU!
AND YOU'LL BE SORRY IF YOU FLOAT!
COME...
YOUR BROOM...
THERE. THIS IS OLD MAN MATTHEW'S ORCHARD.
GET RID OF HIM FOR US... THE DRAGON, NOT THE OLD MAN...
MIND YOU...
WE'LL FORGET YOUR LITTLE... LET'S SAY... SLEIGHTS OF HAND!
IF YOU SUCCEED!
WE'LL LEAVE YOU TO IT!
YOU'RE TOO KIND!
ROOOAA
GOOD THING THIS DIDN'T DRAG ON, IF I DARE SAY SO...
BUT... WHAT'S HE DOING?
I'LL FOLLOW HIM!
HE'S FLYING TOWARDS THE BLACK MOUNTAINS...
HERE WE ARE.

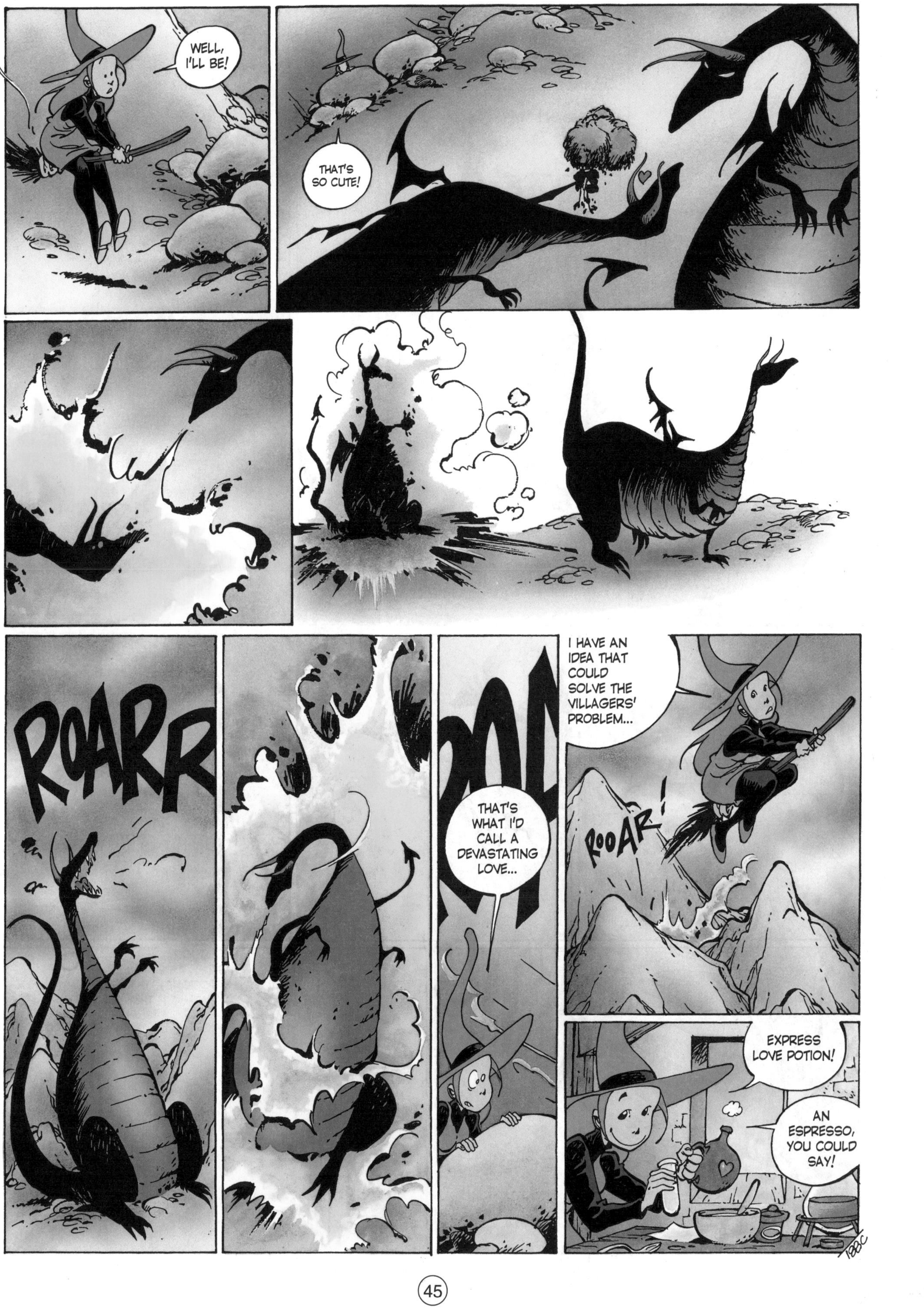
WELL, I'LL BE!
THAT'S SO CUTE!
ROARR
THAT'S WHAT I'D CALL A DEVASTATING LOVE...
I HAVE AN IDEA THAT COULD SOLVE THE VILLAGERS' PROBLEM...
ROOAR!
EXPRESS LOVE POTION!
AN ESPRESSO, YOU COULD SAY!

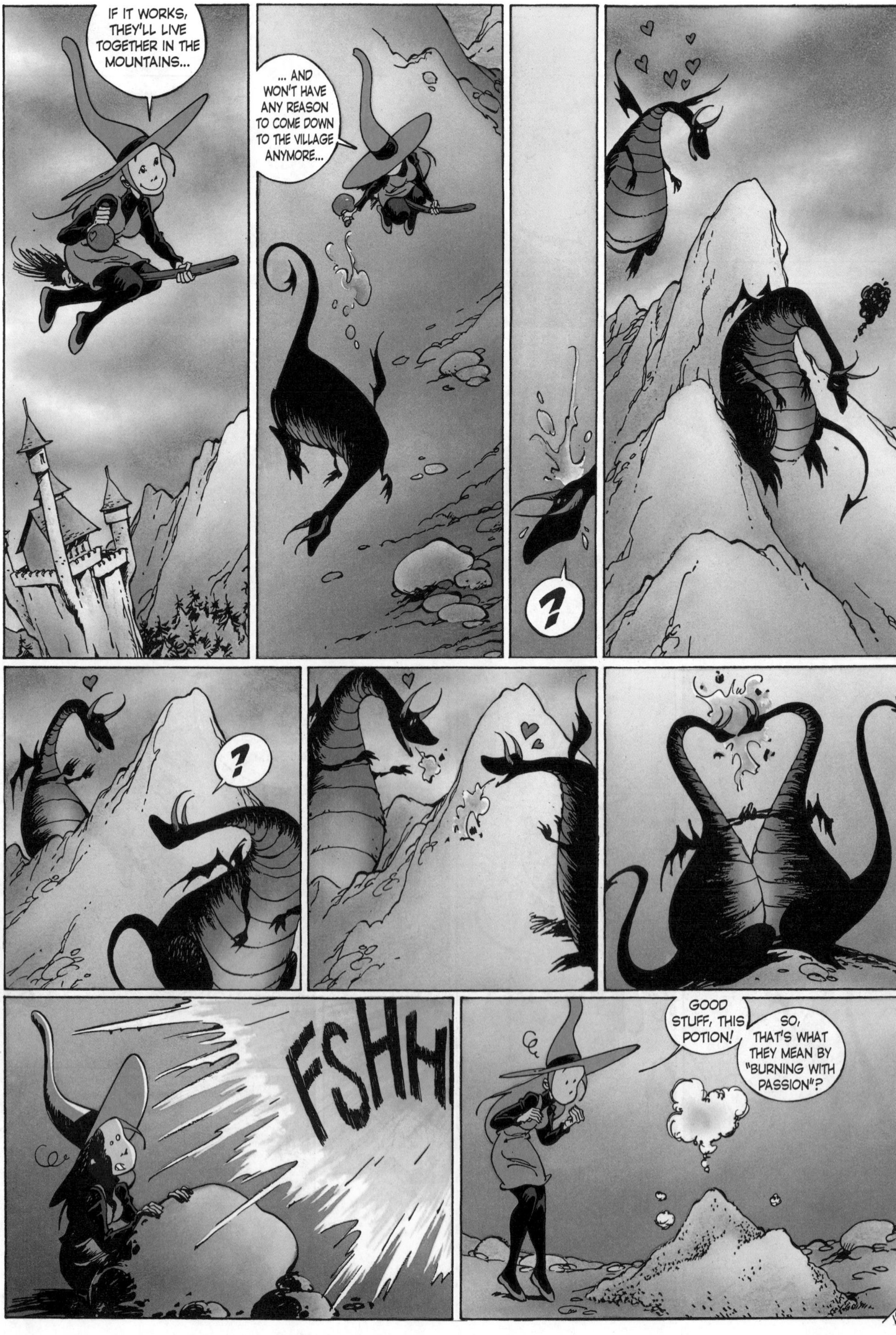

IF IT WORKS, THEY'LL LIVE TOGETHER IN THE MOUNTAINS...
... AND WON'T HAVE ANY REASON TO COME DOWN TO THE VILLAGE ANYMORE...
?
?
FSHH
GOOD STUFF, THIS POTION!
SO, THAT'S WHAT THEY MEAN BY "BURNING WITH PASSION"?
GILSON • CLARKE • CERISE

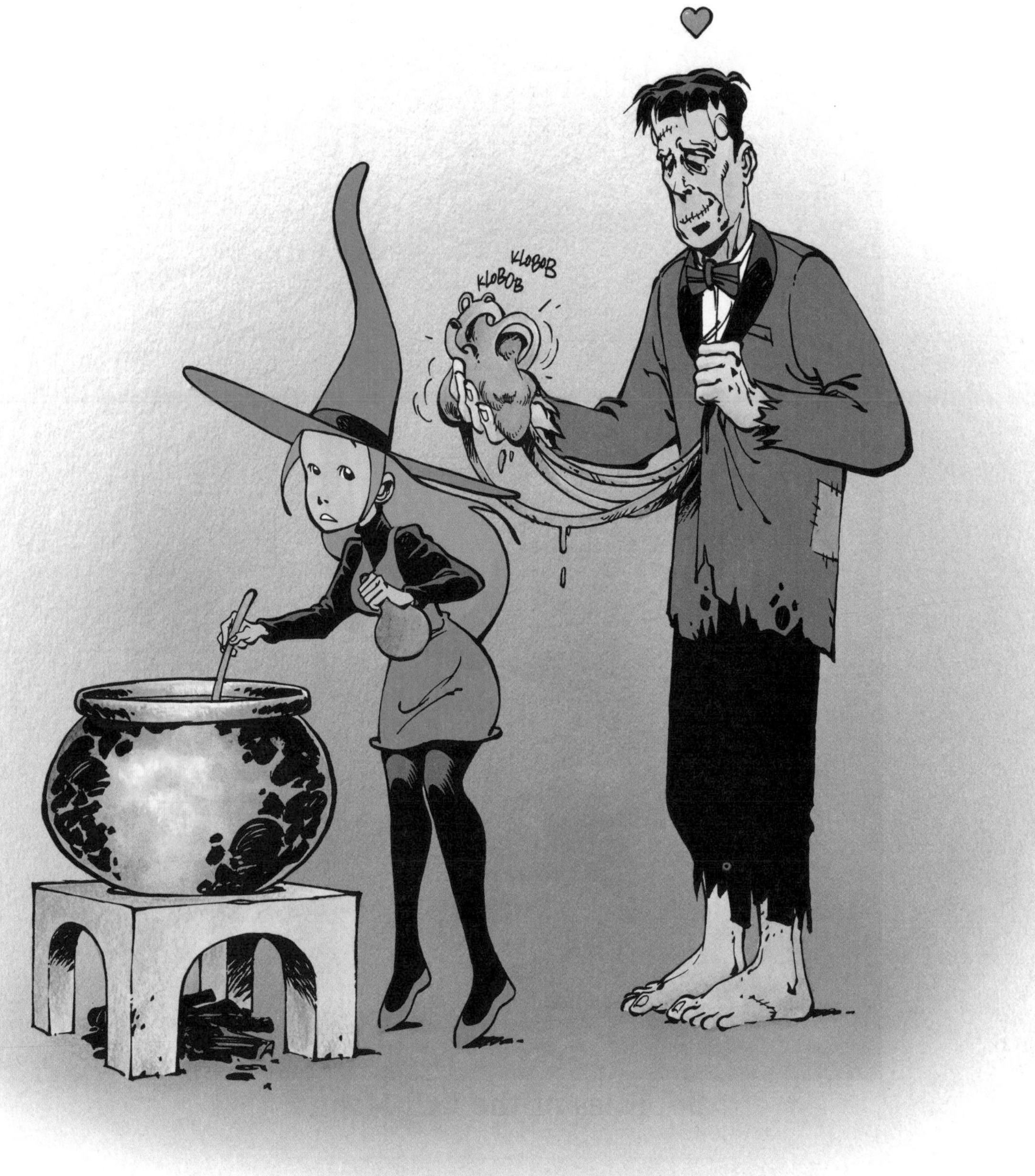
KLOBOB
KLOBOB

Coming soon

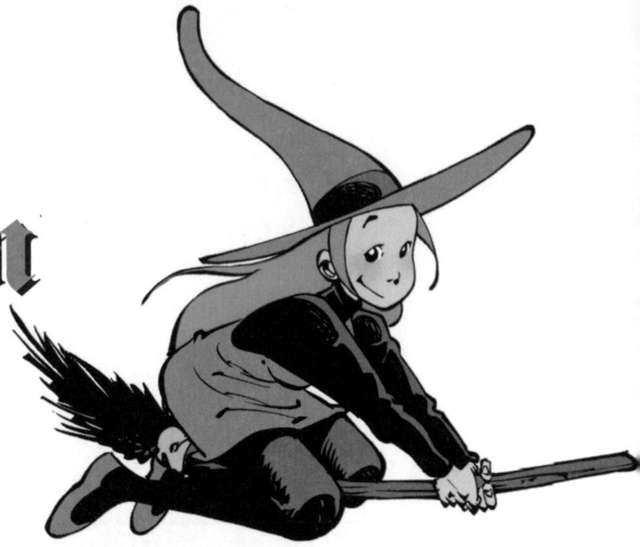

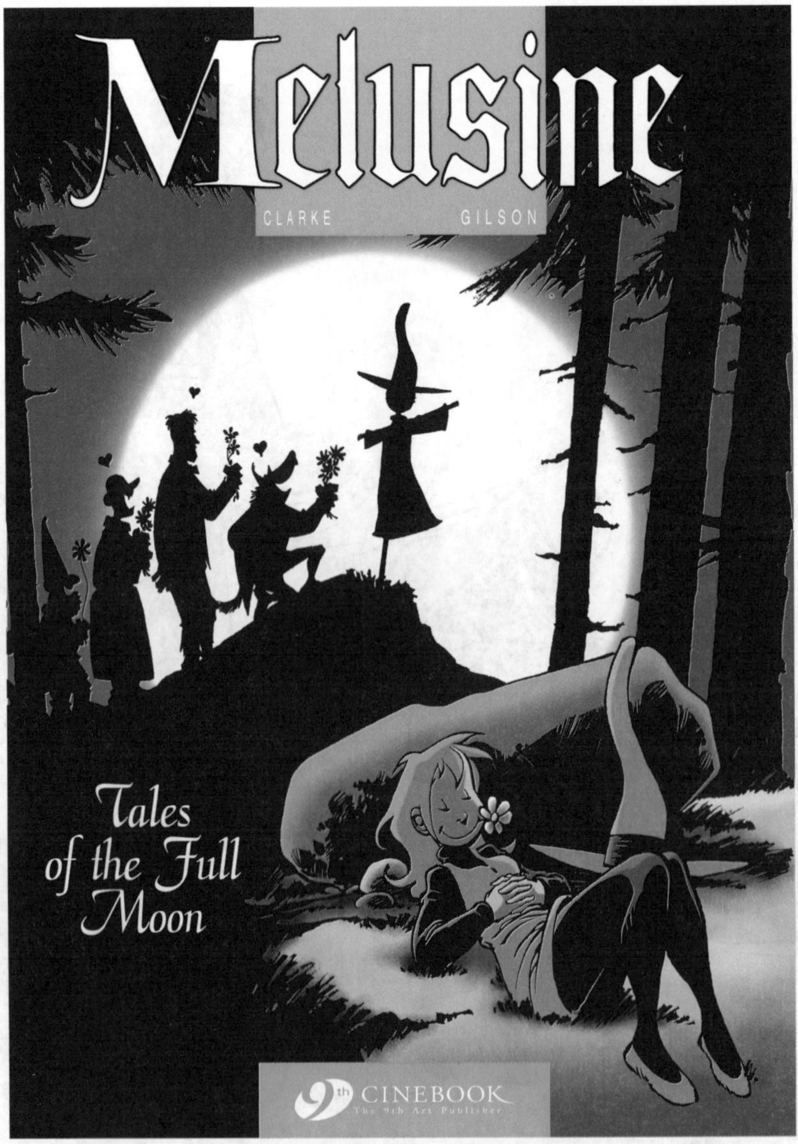

Melusine
CLARKE
GILSON
Tales of the Full Moon
CINEBOOK
The 9th Art Publisher

5 - Tales of the Full Moon

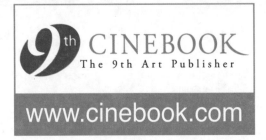